Island, Love & Fate

by
Miya Kwen

Published by Icons Media Publishing in 2024

First Edition

TABLE OF CONTENTS

PROLOGUE

The icy water shocks her system as she plunges beneath the surface of the ocean. she felt nothing, nothing but pain as the water squeezed the breath out of her. Her body was numb. She couldn't move or feel her body. Why can't she move? Why was she so weak? She could see the reflected light above which faded slowly as her body drowned in the dark, so was her hope of survival. No one was coming. No one was coming to save her as usual. it is finally going to be over. All those years of sadness loneliness and depression will finally come to an end. Who knew she would die like this, she would finally have peace. Who knew dying felt so cold and painful? Or was it because of the water?

****

8 hours earlier

" Daddy please I'm sorry " the little girl cried for mercy as her father dragged her to the bedroom. Struggling and fighting for freedom knowing very well it was of no use.

" I said shut up " he yells as he throws her on top of the bed.

"Daddy please " she begged in tears. Just once, just this once he should let her go. The man grabs his belt, panting like he just finished hard labour. " Daddy " ignoring her plea, ties her hand to the bed and leans forward.

" come on sweetheart. Why are you doing this to me " adjusting her messy hair. Long and black. Just like her mothers." you know I love you " he whispers to her ear as she sob. " I love you so much "

" Daddy please " watching the man pull himself up and take off his trousers " Daddy no, daddy no " crying as loud as she could for someone to come rescue her.

" Brrrrrrrrrrrrrrrrrrrr " the sound of the ringing alarm filled the air pulling her out of her nightmare.

" h, h,h,h,h " panting and sweating " h,h,h " using her right hand to massage her forehead and the other to wipe the tears that she only just noticed. " hh it was just another one" whispers while she reached for her phone to turn off the alarm.

Lara, A 26 years old, tall, perfect wavy black hair and dark skin. Always carrying a blank expression. She makes her way downstairs to grab a glass of water in the kitchen. Lara puts the empty glass down while she scrolls through her emails trying to distract herself from the nightmare she had earlier. The nightmares have been going on for 10 years now. Nothing new, just that same nightmare. She thought that it would be over once she left that place and started afresh, but she was wrong. Her past has continued to hunt her to this day. " Damn I need those pills " says to herself. The doctor told her she has PTSD (post-traumatic stress disorder) so she takes pills to ease her nerves. Suddenly a message from Mr James pops up, asking for her to come to his office, issues about her new script.

Dressed in a luxurious white suit and pair of white heels. Lara walks into the industry with full confidence, ignoring the greetings of other employees. She entered the elevator and headed straight for the CEO's office.

" Lara!" Mr James greeted me with a welcoming smile " you are right on time " Mr James, An average height, plump, with bark hair, dark brown eyes and a charming smile. His love for money, limitless. Which makes Lara one of his favourite person

"Good morning to you to James" giving him that lifeless smile. He gestures for her to take a sit across his table.

" come, sit down " He watches Lara walk towards the chair and sit down, placing her purse on her thigh. " so Lara " he began after she settled " I read the treatment and as always, it is splendid " he compliments with a smile which faded almost immediately as it appeared " but... " he hesitates

" but what " with a bit of curiosity in her tone

" the ending " Lara instantly rolls her eyes. " we have talked about this over and over again. Your work is great but the ending is always a problem. Fans are beginning to complain "

" there is nothing wrong with the ending Mr James " sounding calm as she speaks

" The script is not going to sell "

" that is what you say but it always does " she reminded

" not this time. Like I said, people are beginning to complain and if you don't do something about it. it will affect your status." they were both taken by silence. "hh" he sighed as he leaned forward in his chair with hands on the table, fingers locked " Lara..."

" let's face the reality" she cuts him off " Is there ever truly a happy ending " looking into his dark brown eyes waiting for an answer

" don't forget this is the entertainment industry. We create stories that bring smiles to the audience's faces and stories that make them happy. love, fantasy, romance, comedy and sometimes we give them action and tragedy. They don't want reality, they want a happy ending because that gives them hope.."

" lies " cuts him off again " they want lies "

"look Lara " with a seriousness in his tone. Lara quietly watched him open his drawer and bring out that familiar thick envelope. Placing it on the table " this is wonderful but it won't work"

" what! " with a frown

" I want you to write something new, something fresh and exciting. And " he hesitates "A HAPPY ENDING" emphasizing those three words " but before that, you need a vacation "

" No I don't " she debates

" yes you do and I don't care if you want it or not, you are going on a vacation. You need to go somewhere that will lighten you up a little, get some fresh air. I've already prepared a private plane, your secretary Joanna, will bring your luggage. You leave at 1:30 pm

" where " with a reluctant tone

" you are going back to Nigeria "

" Ee " with eyes wide open, completely shocked at the name of the Country he mentioned " Why Nigeria " trying to remain calm

" for goodness sake Lara when was the last time you visited home? It's been 10 years " he marks " you have to go see your people, your home "

home?. Thinking. That is not home and will never be home. That is the past life she left behind and promised never to return to. The life that still hunts her to this day.

" Mr James, I am sorry but..."

" no buts, you are going home. How long you stay depends on you " not giving her a chance to finish her sentence " Come on Lara. Go home, meet them and set whatever happened between you and them straight. Go and lighten up your mood. Sometimes I wonder if you know the feeling of happiness at all "

****

" Happiness" She whispers as she walks out of the office. What does it feel like again? She wonders. Lara couldn't remember the last time she felt genuinely happy. Now she's going back, back to the place she never wanted to set foot in again.

" Lara?" a familiar voice called from behind, drawing her out of her deep thought. Lara turns around. Completely shocked to see that face

" Davina " the name rolled out off her lips in a questionable manner, not expecting to see her in the industry. What is she doing here? Lara wonders

CHAPTER

1

Lara

The heavy sunlight that reflected through the window hit her eyes as she opened them. At first, her environment was blurred but after a few blinks it became clear. she managed to sit up in bed and her eyes explored the unfamiliar room trying to remember where she was and how she got there. She noticed she had a bandage around her head

" where am I?" the question rolled out of her lips as she looked around. it was a big room, well polished with wooden items of furniture and the walls were painted white. There were a few paintings on the wall and all of them had something to do with the sea. She struggled out of bed feeling a bit dizzy but ignored this. The moment her feet touched the ground, the door opened. A lady walks in. with dark blonde hair, golden eyes and is dressed in a sky-blue dress. She wore a neckless that was made out of tiny sea shells and was holding a bowl of water

" oh" eyes wide open" Thank goodness you are awake" she had a very charming voice and Lara was certain that she hadn't seen her before

" and you are?....." trying to get her identity

" Cordelia" she carried a warm smile as she introduced herself. Lara watches as she walks up to the table and places the bowl of water on it" so how are you feeling?"

" I don't know" she responded honestly trying to remember what happened" What happened?"

" there was a plane crash. My master found you by the ocean bay and rescued you"

" so where am I?"

" Marine island" she replied before taking a few steps towards her immediately Lara stepped back getting the urge to protect herself from the lady in front of her" Oh, sorry"

" Marine island?" the place sounded to unfamiliar to Lara" I have never heard of it"

" that is strange. Marine Island is very well known for a lot of things" in deep thought" where are you from?"

" I'm...." thinking which was odd because she should know where she is from, shouldn't she ?" where am I from?" a confused look on her face as she asked the lady

" how should I know" the lady was also confused by her question" you don't know where you are from ?"

" wait....." realization hit her, that not only does she not remember where she was from. she also does not remember who she was" what is my name?" she asked almost panicking

" OK. something is wrong. I will get the doctor. Don't leave this room" instructs and with that Lara watched the lady run out of the room leaving her in a confused state. What is happening? Why can't I remember anything? She sat back down as her head began to ache, feeling dizzy" What is th..is ?" her voice cracked

****

" well she is fully recovered" the doctor announced as he finished examining Lara. Cordelia who looked really worried stood beside the doctor.

" if she is fully recovered, why can't she remember who she is ?"

" she did hit her head pretty hard in the crash. And adding to the shock of the entire situation. I will say she has Amnesia" he says

" Amnesia?" with an eye brow raised" what is that ?"

" memory loss" he says in simpler words

" So will I get my memories back ?" eyes focused on the doctor. A man in his mid-fifties, dark green eyes and dark blond hair which were already turning grey

" it depends. If we can find something that triggers her memories. Maybe something from her past life" the doctor explained while he packed up

" and where can we get something from my past life when I can't even remember a single thing?" She frowned at the situation. Lara couldn't believe that she lost her memory. The memories of her own self. She couldn't remember a single thing, even where she lived or at the least her name and she felt frustrated

" This is not good" Cordelia speaks in a low tone

" I will take my leave" the doctor announced as he grabbed his fully packed bag from the corner and left Cordelia and Lara alone. She rested her head on the headboard with her eyes closed as she sighed in frustration. Why did she have to lose her memory on an unknown island

" yes," Cordelia interrupts the silence with a bit of excitement in her tone" The waste from the plane crash. I am sure we can find something there that belongs to you. That may help" Lara gave a small smile at her words, grateful that she was able to come up with such an idea

" that is a splendid idea" sitting up

" I will speak to Malik the moment he returns home but before then you should have a good rest"

" I need a bath. I feel like I haven't had a good bath in weeks"

" that is because you have been out for a week and three days" She was surprised at the sometimes not so surprise" I usually just clean you up with water and cloth.

" I was out for so long and I can't even remember why."

" I will prepare your bath" making her way to the bathroom

" thank you" she said in a low tone that Cordelia couldn't hear

Sitting in the plane alone with her eyes focused on her phone screen. She scrolled through Instagram on the Marvel Studio page. Their latest" BLACK PANTA" will be out soon and suddenly the plane went off balance." o my god" she held on to the chair so she wouldn't fall off while her phone left her hand." what is going on" She called out to anyone. The flight attendant ran towards her panting and she could see the horror in the lady's eyes, immediately She knew something was off

" the pilot, the pilot" finding it difficult to speak with the unstable plane moving them from side to side

" what happens to the pilot"

" the pilot....is..is dead" Her heart sank instantly after hearing these words

" what!!" she panicked as well. If there is no pilot then who is flying the plane? BOOM they heard the sound of one of the engines.

"The plane will crash we have to jump out" she said as she struggled to get off her chair. Suddenly the plane went off again and so did the both of them. Lara didn't know what happened next but all she knew was that her head was in sudden pain. Probably hit it somewhere and everything became a blur

" miss, miss" hears someone's cry and that was it..........

" hhhhhhhh" Lara jumped up to reality, sitting on the bed, panting and sweating. She looks around realizing where she was" It was a dream, it was just a dream" repeating to herself as she slowly clams down. She Used the sleeve of her shirt to wipe out the sweat on her forehead.

Lara got out of bed suddenly needing to drink water. her eyes fell on the wall clock above her bed to see that it was past midnight. Walked up to the door, reached for the handle and opened it. This will be her first time leaving the room. It was dark but only a blind person won't be able to see. She had no idea where she was going but from the level of silence In the house She knew it was a very big house and it would take one a little time to get used to the place. That is if she will be staying long. It all depends on when she gets her memories back. Still trying to figure out her way in the dark hallway she suddenly heard a noise coming from a direction. Lara followed the sound which led her to the kitchen she was looking for.

This was the only part of the house that had lights on, probably because of the unfamiliar guy who was operating his laptop at the table. He lifted his head to acknowledge her presence and Lara was met with strangely attractive ocean-blue eyes. Long honey blond hair which had some in a ponytail while the rest fell to his shoulders and a pleasant smile." hello" his voice was deep and calm and as he stood up you could tell that he was hitting the gym once in a while. And damn, can someone look so presentable in just a simple hoodie and sweatpants?

" hm. Hi?" she gave that lifeless smile she always gave and waved awkwardly." sorry. Who are you ?"

" Malik. My name is Malik" He introduced himself

" oh. You are the one who saved me, aren't you ?"

" yes. How are you feeling" he took a few steps closer

" thank you for saving me" she said ignoring his question. She had to thank him before any other thing. She didn't know why but when Cordelia told her she was saved by someone, she was a bit surprised. Maybe she didn't expect it or maybe it is something else.

" It's something that anyone will do so you do not have to thank me"

" I don't think so" she said.

he raised an eyebrow in confusion" what makes you think that." he had a bit of curiosity in his tone and she shrugged in response" how are you feeling"

" I don't know" Malik didn't say anything after her responses like he was waiting for her to say something more." I honestly don't know. The doctor says that I am fully recovered but I don't feel that way. I can't remember a single thing about me and I feel like I am forgetting something important, that I shouldn't forget."

" oh yes. I am aware of that." Nodding in understanding

"the lady, Cordelia said she would speak to you about..." he cut her off

" yes she did and I am afraid that it won't be possible. The bay has already been cleared out because it will be dangerous to have things like that around and besides I already checked hoping to find a purse or an ID that will tell me about you but it was nothing. Nothing that will be of help to you" She frowned at his words. Does this mean that she is stuck with no memories in this place?

"This is messed up." Looking around in frustration and back at him" what do I do now? I can't remain like this"

" We will find a way" he tries to assure her

" Damn it" She whispers under her breath. Why was he so calm about it?

" but why are you up so late?"

" Couldn't sleep" look down to her feet

" why? Do you have a headache? Or feel dizzy" he took a few more steps closer to cheek if she was alright but she instantly stepped back. From her movement, Malik instantly noticed that she didn't want him to touch her" oh. I'm sorry" stepping back a little

" I had a nightmare that is all. I just wanted to drink water" explaining her reason for being out

" I see" nodding in understanding with a small smile

****

Davina

Los Angeles, California. Hotel room.

Long straight black hair, forest green eyes, perfect glowing skin and perfect body. Davina is sitting on the bed in her hotel room when she gets a call from a strange number. Knowing exactly who it was, She reached for her phone beside her and took the call

" is it done" getting straight to business

" yes. She is dead" the person from the other end speaks

" are you sure it is confirmed" with a serious tone

" yes"

" Good. I will send you your remaining pay" with that she puts an end to the call. Davina walks up to the table and grabs her glass of wine, then she plays her favourite opera which takes over the entire room While Davina dances in victory.

Miya Kwen

CHAPTER
2

Looking out the window. The perfect view before her, she could see the ocean at a good distance and trees of different kinds. The breeze that travelled in through the window messed up her hair but she didn't mind. Enjoying the peace and the calmness of the breeze. In a strange way took her mind away from her current situation. *'knock, knock'*. the knock on the door interrupted. Cordelia walks in with a warm smile, dressed in a yellow dress with flowery patterns all over. The dress she wore said a lot about her gentle personality

" good morning" Cordelia greets

" morning." giving her that lifeless smile which faded immediately while she turned around to face the lady before her

" how are you feeling"

" what should I say? I am fine I guess" crossing her arms

" I spoke to Malik yesterday....."

" He told me" cutting her off" we met last night and he told me"

" Am sorry" sounding a disappointed

" You say sorry like it is your fault" their gaze met" I am fine. I am sure they will return"

" I hope so" biting her lower lips" Let us have breakfast" She wasn't hungry but with the smile the young lady gave, Lara could not say no

" Ok. , give me a few minutes to wash up" Cordelia nodded in understanding and left.

In a few minutes, Lara was walking into the kitchen only to find Cordelia talking to another lady. Their attention was drawn to her the moment she walked in" oh. Have a sit" Cordelia spoke. She makes her way to the seat next to the kitchen island" by the way this is Rebecca. She can be annoying sometimes so don't pay attention to her" Rebecca rolled her eyes at Cordelia's silly words, while she leaned on the island grabbing an apple from the basket of fruits next to Lara

"Don't mind her" she spoke with a beautiful smile displaying her dimples. Rebecca. A beautiful lady with pearl wavy hair and light brown eyes. She had a straight nose and cute lips, her skin was fit for a model and she looked really professional in her medical suit ." you are beautiful" she compliments

" I will say the same to you," Lara says forcing a smile making Rebecca blush

" thank you. I like your dark skin, it's glowy" Lara's eyes fell on her hand as she explored her skin, to her there was nothing really special about it

" thanks"

" I made sandwich" Cordelia announced

" package one for me. I have to leave now, Malik said that the next time I come late it will be a cut from my salary" Rebecca says to Cordelia

" ok"

In silence she watched Cordelia package the sandwich for Rebecca and left in a hurry. Lara turns to Cordelia who just severed her a plate" are they doctors" asked" Malik and Rebecca I mean"

" marine biologies" Cordelia corrected" they watch over the marine island sea"

"oh" nodding

" so what do you plan to do today?" Cordelia's question got her confused

" I don't know" she shrugged

" you have been indoors for too long. Don't tell me you plan to go on like that" Cordelia looked really shocked at her words.

" it doesn't sound like much of a problem" with a little reluctance in her tone

" well today is your lucky day because you happen to be around during one of the most exciting periods in Marine Island"

" what is happing today" reaching for her sandwich

" Today" Cordelia walks round the table excitedly and stood beside her"is the chosen festival" stopping her from dissolving the sandwich

" chosen festival?" with an eyebrow raised

" yes" smiles brightly" it's the festival where the male on the island gets to announce who they want to marry when the time is right and Malik is going to be one of them"

"Who?"

" Malik. Our young master will finally have a bride and I wonder who he has his eyes on"

" oh, I see. That's a pretty fun tradition"nodding her head as she acknowledged

" you don't sound excited or anything"

" sorry if it bothers you but the festival is the least of my problems. And besides I can't get excited about something I know nothing of"

" well you are about to see it for yourself" smiling" Eat up because we are going out" Lara nodded. She wasn't interested in having a debate with the young lady and besides she had nothing to do, no clue of when her memories will return. She can only just participate in whatever these people do until she remembers something.

****

She changed into a simple top and trousers. Cordelia offers her a black P Cap and leads her out of the house. Lara was stunned by the perfect view, it was one beautiful island and where the house stood one could see everything below. She suddenly got this urge to go down and explore the place.

" Wait here" Cordelia says to her and trailed off to who knows where. Turning around her eyes travelled around her environment. Suddenly she caught the attention of a mansion at the very top of the island. It was surrounded by tall trees hiding most part of the mansion but anyone could tell how massive it was. Her curiosity took over her as she stared at it, wondering who owned such a building.

Cordelia suddenly appeared riding a red convertible which stopped beside her. She took off her sunglasses and smiled brightly" What do you think ?" seeking a compliment.

" not bad" she said plainly. Cordelia frowned

" not bad?" with an eyebrow raised

" what responses were you expecting ?"

" I don't know but I wasn't expecting Not bad." she says honestly." never mind, gets in"

****

In a few seconds, we were driving off, down to the island. Cordelia was more excited than Lara was. The lower we got the more interesting the place became. it looked like a work of art like she was stuck in a world of painting, the trees, flowers, The bright sky, and fresh air. It felt perfect. As they drove, the breeze blew so hard that she had to take off her P cap so it wouldn't fly off. It messed up my hair but she didn't mind." Welcome to Marine Island" Cordelia spooked proudly as they finally got to the main town and it was a busy one.

Lara noticed the people's outfits. The women were dressed in long flay dresses of different colours but all had one thing in common, signs of waves and boats were knitted around it, And their jewellers were all made of sea shells like the one Cordelia had, not to forget their hair which was decorated with different hairpins. The men on the other hand all wore ocean blue kaftan and very loose trousers.

" why the sea shells ?" with curiosity in her tone

" pardon ?"

" that" her eyes fell on the neckless around Cordelia's neck

" oh this" Cordelia smiles. She didn't respond immediately. Cordelia parked in front of a salon, which on the billboard says '*Madam V's styling*'. Immediately Cordelia turns off the engine and turns to her" this is like a reminder that wherever we go we should always remember who we are and where we are from, our history and home"

" oh" with her eyes on the neckless, she thought about herself. Does she have something like this as well, something that will remind me of who she was and where she's from? something that will remind her of her home. Did she even have a home? Lost in her thought

" Cordelia !!!" a woman's voice calls, pulling her out of her deep thoughts. She was the owner of the shop they parked in front of and Lara had no idea when a woman came out

"Madam V" Cordelia called back while getting out of the car" Hohandara Madam V" she greeted in a strange language as they hugged. Lara quietly got out of the car while she watched the two talk in that language for a little while before giving her their attention

" who is she?"

" oh, this......." Cordelia stops for a while as she realises that Lara doesn't have a name" this is my friend Guinevere" suddenly giving her a name which took her by surprise

" oh my God, that is a lovely name" Madam V walks up to her. She was about to step back but didn't get a chance. She pulls her in for a very strong hug that almost suffocated her" it is nice having you here. I had no idea we would be having a visitor" she says after pulling away. Madan V looks up at due to the height difference. Madam V was a short and plump dark lady with very curly hair and dark brown eyes" and a beautiful one for that matter" compliments Lara

" thank you" Lara gives a soft smile as she acknowledges her compliment

" so what are you doing in Marine Island?" with confusion written in Lara's eyes, she looks at Cordelia hoping she bills her out of the question

" oh. She came to attend the Island's festival, I have told her all about it and she would like to see it for herself"

" that is great" the woman smiled" That means you will be staying for a while... it also so means that you will be coming to my salon soon, there is a lot to tell about this Isla....."

"All alright Madan V we have to go now" Cordelia interrupted as she took Lara's hand away from the woman's grip

" so fast? But you just got here" disappointment flashed in her eyes

" I promise I will bring her back but for now, I have a lot to show her, I just said I should introduce her to you first after all you are the most special person in my heart" Madam V blushed at Cordelia's words, while Lara found it really cute

" OK then. I will be waiting" she waves them goodbye while Cordelia pulls Lara along with her. Cordelia didn't slow down on till the salon was out of sight

" are you running away from her ?" the confused lady had to ask while forcing her hand out of Cordelia's grip "oh sorry" letting her go" no and yes. Madam V always have something to say, she can hold someone for more than an hour especially if it is a new face that is why I had to take you away"

" oh" nodding in understanding.

****

For the next few hours, Cordelia showed her around the Island. It became clear to Lara that Cordelia was famous on the island because they always had someone stopping them midway to say hi and they were all very nice and friendly. It is a place where everyone knows everyone and their outfit makes the entire place colourful.

" so is this how everyone on the island usually dresses, so traditional"

" why do you ask? You don't like it ?" with an eyebrow raised still focused on driving. It was almost sunset and they were heading to who knows where.

" I kind of do" looking around

" you don't look like you do" Lara turns to her. Giving her a confused look" I don't see the excitement on your face

"Does it have to be on my face"

" for normal people? Yes ." she gave her a quick look before focusing back on the road once again" I showed you all the most interesting places on the island and all your comments were, ' It's nice ', interesting, it's good"

" what should I say"

" show me that you have interest in the whole thing. Do you know how excited tourist get when we take them to those places during their tour? but you just gave a plain expression"

" but I indeed love the tour"

" well, you didn't show me any sign that you did. Were you a sadist in your past life or something?"

" well I won't know, I can't remember anything. By the way, where is everyone heading" she noticed that everyone was heading in the same direction as they were

" to the place of the festival" smiles" Cordelia lifts her right hand to point at the mansion at the top of the island, the mansion that she once wondered who owned" that is the home of the chief"

" the Chief ?" with an eyebrow raised

" yes. The fishers, they are the founder of this island and also Malik's family" she explained

" Malik's family own this place?" surprised while Cordelia nodded at her question" so they are like king and queen ?"

" yeah but we use Chiefs and besides they preferred to be called the fishers"

" I see" nodding

" trust me, you will enjoy the festival" she looks her way briefly before focusing on the road again" this island knows how to welcome new people"

" I have notice" she says as her mind goes back to how everyone greeted her back in the town and they all seemed to like her dark skin which made me a bit uncomfortable, not to forget the amazed look in their eyes when Cordelia said her name was Guinevere" what does Guinevere mean?"

" white wave" she says calmly

" why did you name me that?" curiously

" Why? you don't like it?"

" am just curious, why? and also I am black"

" the name has nothing to do with your colour, it's just what came to my head as I looked at you. it suite you"

"How?"

" damn, you ask a lot of questions" she laughs out loud

"*Guinevere*" Lara whispered the name under her bright and felt strangely nice," I like the name" settling into her seat, making herself comfortable

Miya Kwen

CHAPTER

3

In less than an hour, they were heading towards the mansion with the sun already set. from where they were Lara could tell that it was a castle and a beautiful one. There were tons of cars packed on the way. People got out of their cars to walk. Thinking Cordelia would do the same, instead, she drove straight for the castle forcing people to make way so they wouldn't get hit. She expected them to get upset by Cordelia's action but they weren't, they just greeted each other loudly with bright smiles.

They got to the gate. The moment Cordelia's car is sported by the securities, the gate is opened wider. The security guards greeted them as they drove in and Lara only wondered who Cordelia was to this people.

" and here we are" Cordelia announced while getting out. Lara followed and watched Cordelia hand the key over to a young man who got into the car and drove off.

Lara stood speechlessly amazed by the beauty of her environment. it was more than she imagined it to be like from where she stared at it earlier today. Not knowing if it was the night that made the place this beautiful or it was just this beautiful. One could stay here all day and never get bored" are you smiling right now" Cordelia looked amazed for some strange reasons

" Pardon" with an eyebrow raised

" you were smiling just now" still amazed" and it suits you"

" oh" nodding

" and you just killed it" she rolled her eyes.

The compound was well decorated with flowers, and balloons and the people looked so colourful as they walked around in their traditional outfits. She spotted a kid running off with his mother running after him" Imran came back here" she calls, running after the child with anger written on her face

"Only the lord can save that woman" Cordelia says from behind her. Lara turns to see that she is also focused on the same woman who was after her child

" why do you say that"

" she has 9 boys, she shouts every day and night, running after one now and the other later"

" that is tragic"

" no it is not" using her eyes to follow the woman who just caught the child by the ear and dragged him along with her" it may look tragic from the outside but when you go into the family you will see the love between them" as she spoke Lara watches the two quietly wondering what it was like back with her own family, the family that she can't even remember now. She felt pain in her chest at the thought

" ah" a silent gasp of pain escaped her lips

"Are you alright" both interrupted by that familiar male voice. Malik. She lifted her head to see his eyes on her, with a concerned look" are you in pain of any kind" standing in front of her and she gave a fake smile

" I am fine" he stares at her for a while not believing

" Are you sure"

" Yeah"trying to convince him Malik nods slightly at her responses

" why are you two still here, let's go to the back" he says not getting his eyes off her

" won't you dress up" Cordelia says with an eyebrow raised" today is your day remember"

" My day and many other guys" corrects her

" well they will definitely be dressed by now, I can't let my beloved cousin dress like this for this day, you have to stand out from all the rest"

" wait, Cousin?" Lara, completely taken aback

" yes," she responded" Malik and I are cousins. Distant cousins"

" then why do you call him master"The young lady just shrugs at her question

" she does that. I have tried talking her out of it but for some reason, she just enjoys doing so" Malik explained with that warm smile" you two also need to change"

" our outfit is not important, yours is. And by the way who will be the lucky girl" wiggling her eyebrow

" I don't know, the matchmaker will decide" shrugs

" you still don't have anyone in mind" Cordelia crossed her arms like she was interrogating him

" I do, it's just that" his eyes fell on Lara" It will be strange asking her to marry me. She will certainly say no" Lara raised an eyebrow at him

" oh I see" she turns to Cordelia who was now giving an awkward smile

" what ?" totally lost in the sibling's conversation

" Nothing, lets go change" she takes Lara's hand. Immediately Lara pulls her hand away" oh so sorry" feeling guilty

" no, it is not a problem" Lara felt nervous all of a sudden

"let's go" calmly, Malik says using his hand to gesture to her the way, while trying to avoid touching her.

They both lead her into the house. The house was stunning, with classic furnitures, and beautiful paintings as they walked through the hallway with Lara behind them. She noticed all the family photos on the wall, from the first generation to the present and she sported a photo of only Malik in a graduation gown from high school. He looked really cute and his hair was much shorter back then.

****

Cordelia helped her in the traditional outfit. A white long sleeved, flay gown which had blue wave patterns knitted around it, the sleeve was made of lase and the tip of the gown also had lase. her hair was nicely done and different hair pins were used to decorate it.

Cordelia wore a dark green dress with white patterns around it and her hair was made just like Lara's." you look beautiful" Lara complimented

" if you say am beautiful what will I say about you? You look just so perfect in that dress"

" thanks"

" are your parent mixed by any chance" She frowns at Cordelia's question

" how will I know"

" sorry" bit her lower lips, feeling guilty"forgot. come on let's go, the festival is about to start" She leads her out of her room, out of the house but this time to the massive backyard.

The backyard was crowded with men, women and children, several large tables had varieties of food. Music instruments played, taking over the entire place and in the middle of the whole activities were 15 chairs facing 1 chair

" what is that for" pointing to the chairs

" oh that" Cordelia smiled" There 15 single ladies are going to sit down and that is where the young man will sit for his bride to be chosen.

" oh" on the other side was a burning fire going on and slowly people were beginning to gather around it.

"Let go to the burning fire, the dancers are about to perform" Cordelia says" Can I" seeking permission to take her hand. Lara hesitates and Instead takes Cordelia's hand. She felt comfortable being the one to reach out first, not knowing why but it appears that way. Cordelia drags her along with her as they push through the crowd, everyone in a hurry to get to burn fire. suddenly they both lost contact, disappearing from each other's sight." Cordelia" she called, how could she just leave her like this? looking around to find her in the crowd almost panicking. She followed the crowd heading towards the burn fire maybe she would see her there." ah" a gasp escaped her lips as she tripped, her face almost coming in contact with the ground. sudden someone caught her arm pulling her back up and she was met with does familiar attractive ocean-blue eyes which looked concerned about her

" are you alright?"

" oh" standing properly so she wouldn't fall again, she looked up at him and their gaze met" yes, yes am fine"

" thank goodness," the relief in his eyes was very obvious" Oh am sorry" quickly let go of her hand, as he remembered that she didn't want to be touched" am so sorry. I just didn't want you to fall and..."

" it's fine. I should be thanking you" cutting him off

" oh" relief in his eyes once again

" my face would have hit the ground if it wasn't for you. So thank you"

" welcome" smiled" are you looking for someone?"

" Cordelia, I suddenly lost her"

" don't worry, she will certainly be at the burn fire" with eyes in the direction of the burn fire. her eyes scanned his outfit. He White Kaftan and a loose white trouser which had blue patterns around it like hers and a black scarf around his waist. his outfit was like every other male's outfit. But for reasons she do not know of, he looked Damn good in his. Most of his hair was in a ponytail while the rest at the back fell to his shoulders and some strings of hair at the front fell to his face. Lara's eyes followed as the breeze made it brush his lips

"your outfit is nice" taking her eyes away from his lips

" come on. It is just like everyone else's"

" it is but you look really good in it" he gave her this I can't believe you just said that look and smiled

" thanks"

" let head there" she says pointing to the direction of the burn fire

CHAPTER

4

Standing side by side, they watched the dancers' splendid performance. The ladies looked so beautiful in their dress and as they moved with the flow of the music. Malik leaned down severally to whisper to her ear, how the dance came about and what it meant. If there is one thing she has noticed about these people is that whatever they do has a meaning and it is always something interesting.

The music came to an end. The people cheered the dancers and almost immediately another music started. it was something much crazier and loud, taking everyone with excitement as many joined in, dancing around the fire like it was their last night" oh Guinevere" that familiar voice interrupted" I was looking for you" she turned to look at Cordelia standing beside her looking

excited as well

" you left me" she spoke

" it wasn't in my intention" Cordelia says lifting a finger in defence" and I thought you were the one who let me go" She looks away and her eyes fell on the crowd" Let's join in"

" I don't think I can dance"

" well you won't know until you try" Malik tilted his head to the side as spoke to her

" yeah" Cordelia supported

" I don't feel like dancing" She says not feeling comfortable about joining the crowd. She could see that everyone was having fun which doesn't mean that she would too. Being around so many people felt discomforting enough, she had no intention of making it worst

" alright then" Cordelia pulled Malik's arm

" oh lord" taking him by surprise as Cordelia dragged him into the dance.

She watches them dance together carrying bright smiles on their faces. out of nowhere, Rebecca joined in, taking Malik's hand so they dance together leaving Lara confused as to where she came out from. Throwing their body from side to side.

After a long while of watching. Malik's eyes suddenly fell on her and he winked. Malik let go of Rebecca's hand only to notice him walking up to her. stood in front of her and offered his hand for her to take making her raise an eyebrow in confusion" I said I don't want to dance"

" is it that you don't like fun or you just don't like happiness" looking her in the eyes while he spoke.

"*Happiness*" she repeats under her breath. The word gave her this feeling of familiarity

" come on. Join in"

" I can't dance"

" you won't know that" taking her hand without her concert

" no,no,no,no" he pulls her into the dance floor laughing

" just move along with the music" says out loud so she would hear.

Still holding her hand he moved her from side to side, forcing the dance out of her

" Malik stop this" frowned, but he didn't seem to mind

" move your body to the music" he continued until she finally gave in. In a short while, Lara was in shock to find herself actually moving to the flow of the music, dancing" I told you" sounding proud of his achievement and she found myself smiling back at him. He didn't let go of her hand, nor did she let go of his, they just danced together, jumping and spinning around, forgetting that she was surrounded by people, forgetting everything around her. The music washed everything away like a spell

What was this feeling? She thought to herself when the dance was finally over. What is this strange feeling? Is it the happiness he was talking about or was she just having fun? Whatever it was, she liked it" Are you alright" Malik's voice interrupted her deep thought.

" pardon?" coming back to reality

" you look lost. Is something bothering you?"

" no, not at all"

"Whatever, the chosen is about to start" Rebecca speaks out of nowhere as she pulls Malik along with her

" she is right" Cordelia supported.

****

They gathered around the area. A man and a woman walked out of the mansion with a very old woman behind them. The two looked like couples that had long been married and as they walked, they walked with grace and power, with shoulders upright, and head forward. The people made way for them to walk into the circle

" Malik's parent and the matchmaker" Cordelia whispers to her ear

" oh" Staring at the two, noticing the resemblance. The woman had well-maintained honey blond hair and deep ocean blue eyes like Malik's, she could see where his looks came from, tall and slim, Carried a stunning smile that could brighten anyone's day. The man on the other hand also had dark hair but you will find most of it turning grey and his eyes were dark drown, tall and well built.

" I see the resemblance" whispering back to Cordelia

" Today is another day of the year" the man began" The day that single men of this great island will meet their mate. And we all know how this works don't we? The man will call the name of the woman he has in mind and the matchmaker" the old woman who steps forward as her title is called upon" will check to see if the two will make a good match but if not the matchmaker will give me his true mate"

" And not to forget that today is the day, that the island's future chief, my son" The woman spoke proudly" Will get his bride. And to be honest I can't wait to see who my future daughter-in-law will be" The crowd laughed at her words

" OK. let the event begin" spreading out his hand to start the chosen event.

The event began. Lara who was now interested in this event tried pushing forward through the crowd to get to the front. She watched as the group of girls sat down. Then an unfamiliar guy came out and sat on the single chair in front of them. The matchmaker spread a cloth on the ground. Sitting down she brought out a small metal bow, Lara watched the old woman pour red wine into the bow or was it something else? She had no idea. gently arranging sones around the bow in a zigzag pattern. She spoke a few words in the tribe that Lara did not understand then turned to the young man

" say her name" sounding serious and dangerous

the man smiled and his eyes landed on a young lady amongst the ladies seated

" Sara" out loud. The old woman shouts a few words while looking at the dark sky she looks back down at the metal bow of wine and then whispers a few more words. There was silence for a short while. Watching the old woman, she closed her eyes like she was listening to the red liquid speak. Finally opens the eyes and then smiles." Daniel and Sara are a match" the crowd cheered immediately it was announced" You two will have a lot of children, the last child will be the most suborn but you will manage. You will grow old together and watch your children also get married. Congratulations" she said. Daniel ran to take his feature wife in his arms and the crowd clapped.

"The power of love" Cordelia said out loud as they watched the 5thperson get his mate. Lara just rolled her eyes in response. The word love didn't really go down well with her for reasons she knows not of. The next person was the first not to have any woman in mind. The Matchmaker announced that his mate comes from far away. As far as Egypt and also gave him her name and where to find her.

" is what she says accurate" sounding unconvinced. She didn't believe that anyone was capable of `telling such things

" always" Cordelia says while adjusting her hair which bothered her eyes

" I don't believe her"

" The matchmaker is always right, there have been a few people on the island that went against her and married someone else and it didn't turn out right"

" I still don't believe her"

" understandable"

Beginning to get bored of watching all the love birds and wanted to leave. They had just finished with the 15th guy when it got to Malik's turn. All the girls settled, even Rebecca"Malik and Rebecca in a relationship?"

" nope, childhood friends" Cordelia responded casually. Lara watched the woman repeat the same process then she turned to Malik

" say her name" the matchmaker instructed

" I don't have one" he says and the crowd gasps in shock

" they seriously had to be dramatic about the whole thing" Cordelia rolled her eyes at the crowd's reaction" Not like they don't already know"

" do you have anyone in mind" the matchmaker asked. Malik's eyes suddenly fell on Lara instantly their gaze met

" uuuu" Cordelia mocked into her ear" he has you in mind"

" Don't be ridiculous" she frowns giving Cordelia this cold look

" ok, no offence" she grins, lifting her hands in surrender

" No I don't" Malik turns to the match maker who then nods. Immediately the place was taken by odd silence

Everyone watched the matchmaker as she yelled a few of those same words to the dark sky. then her eyes fell on the metal cup and she whispered a few more words while staring at the cup. She stared at the cup longer than expected then gave a confused look. Lara suddenly felt this strange chill at the back of her neck. like she was being watched. She looked around but no one was looking at her, everyone had eyes on the matchmaker. The matchmaker closed her eyes to listen like she always did, with more seriousness written on her face

"your mate also comes from very far away" Opening her eyes, the matchmaker was amazed" But you are a very lucky man, because she is present in this event" the crowd began to murmur to each other due to the matchmaker's words. The matchmaker stood up and began to walk, using her eyes to explore the girls seated, she looked away from them, then at the crowd. The atmosphere grew intense. As she looked into the crowd searching for the one that will be Malik's mate

"This is getting interesting" Cordelia sounded excited. Walking past several ladies and *Boom*. The old woman's eyes suddenly fell on her. everything felt like a horror movie. She began to regret why she stood at the front or why she even attended the festival. She watches her slowly lift her finger, pointing it at her.

" you are his mate" the words rolled out of her lips taking Lara by surprise.

" me?" she pointed to herself in shock, instantly noticing the people's eyes on her. She moved to the left hoping that maybe the matchmaker was mistaken but her fingers followed" no, no it must be a mistake" she shaking her head

" do you want to run away from your fate" the woman frowned

" I don't believe in fate" said back

" then what do you believe in" an eyebrow raised

" I don't know, and I don't care. But I know that you are mistaken right now"

" I had a feeling it would be you, too" Cordelia said to her

" you are not helping right now miss" starting to get angry

" it must be a mistake" she announced to everyone as they refused to take their eyes off her

" Who is she any way" a voice spoke from being

" I don't even know who I am OK, it is a mistake" yelled getting really uncomfortable with the way people were looking at her

" she is going to be the feature chief's wife" another voice said

" no am not"

" I know her" another voice said" She is a friend of Cordelia's, her name is Guinevere" announced

" Yes I remember her as well" more people began to speak from the crowd. At that moment it felt like the world around her was spinning, every eye on her, whispering and beginning to make her dizzy. The feeling felt familiar, it was something she had experienced before she could tell. From the corner of her eyes, she saw Malik who looked as surprised as she was, walking towards her in a hurry. the matchmaker still didn't stop pointing at her, if only she could bite that finger off. People stared like they had just seen a ghost.

Malik walked past the matchmaker, the moment to reached her he took her hand and began leading out of the crowd. Cordelia followed behind them and together we walked into the mansion

"Are you alright" he asked the moment we were inside standing by the hallway. she stood in front of him with anger written all over her face

" No, I am not. Go tell them that this is a mistake. That matcher maker is lying" she said trying to put myself under control

" The matchmaker does not lie, whatever she says always works out" Cordelia interrupted

" Don't let me pour my anger on you" she snapped

" sorry" Cordelia surrendered noticing how furious the lady before her was

" I will see to the matter. OK" Malik says in his calming tone with both hands on her shoulders" OK" trying to calm her down and to her surprise, it was working

" OK" She nodded in response

"Alright, Cordelia take her home, you need rest" he instructed

" yes master" Cordelia grins while Malik rolls his eyes

" I will see you in the house" with that he walked away

" today will never be forgotten" Cordelia spoke loudly

CHAPTER

5

S itting by the window looking outside. Lara found it difficult to forget about last night. Why is this happening to her? first a plane crash then her memories now she is being mated to the future chief. She has to get out of the island as soon as possible before this gets out of hand. But where will she go? She needs to remember something to know where to go" this is not good" whispered under her breath. She hasn't seen Malik since last night which was for the best but she hopes he has clarified things.

Lara left her room to go get water. She had been in the room all morning and didn't plan on dying out of thirst on an island which is surrounded by water. She made her way to the sitting room and of all people to find in the house she wasn't expecting that beauty," Rebecca?" with an eyebrow raised wondering what she was doing in the house

" if it isn't the future wife of the future chief" giving her this look like she was about to strangle the life out of her

" please don't call me that" feeling irritated

" oh come on, don't tell me you don't like the title" At that moment Lara noticed that she sounded nothing like the first time they met. She sounded like they both have issues with one another that she wasn't aware of and to be honest Lara didn't care if Rebecca did have issues with her. As long as she knew she didn't do anything to offend the lady, besides the two have spoken just once so surely she didn't do anything wrong.

" I don't like it. For goodness sake I don't know where the hell I am or how I got here, I don't have a single memory about me and just like that I am supposed to get married to this guy and you expect me to like it? Does that even make sense to you"

"To me yes. Anyone will want to marry a person like Malik so I do not believe you." she took a few steps forward with a frown" If you truly want to get your memories back how about you go back to how it all started at the ocean"

" Pardon?" not getting her logic

" Go back to the ocean where we found you, drown yourself, I don't care, just leave this island as soon as possible" With that she walked away angrily

" well she woke up on the wrong side of the bed" Lara rolled her eyes. She headed for the kitchen. Helped herself with a glass of water and as she took a gap from it the idea hit her. Rebecca was right. Maybe if she tries to drown herself in the ocean again it will all come back to her.

Lara ran out of the house and began making her way down. She ran past a few people who looked excited to see her and she wondered why. Perhaps it's because she was chosen to be the wife of their future chief. As stupid as it sounds she couldn't believe that they believed what that matchmaker said. The people kept greeting her in a language that she didn't understand and didn't plan on understanding.

Finally coming to a stop she stared at the ocean from far away, knowing that running all the way there would not do her any good if only there was a shorter road. A group of people walked past her and greeted" hohandara future Lady" Lara smiled in response trying as hard as possible to add life to her smiles

" how is your day going my lady?" a young boy stood in front of her out of nowhere, looking up at her as he asked. She flinched in shock

" Oh, heaves" one hand on her chest with eyes wide open. She observed the little boy before her and he smiled brightly, displaying his missing front tooth"ammm..... good?" not sure what to respond," not so good" she said to the boy who now gave her a concerned look

" Why" in his lovely child-like voice, he tilted his head to the side

" I want to get there" pointing to the direction of the ocean

" oh" he smiled

" you know a shortcut?"

" you should have followed the normal road, this is the longest way there" he said

" oh. I thought this was the normal road" she had been running, not certain of the road she was taking all the way, only ended up taking the longer road

" but from here, we can easily get to town and I know a shortcut from there"

" so..." waiting for him to offer his help

" what are we waiting for? let's go" he seemed excited to help.

****

He led her to town and they had to stop to greet a lot of people. Everyone wanted to speak to the future lady. They drew closer to the ocean, she could see it from where she was.

" Thank you for helping me" looking down at the young boy

" don't thank me, thank you" raised an eyebrow in confusion

" Pardon?"

" you have no idea how happy I am to be walking with you, I can't wait for you to become the lady of this island"

" you like me already?" shocked

" why won't I? You are so pretty" she couldn't help but stare at the cute boy, smiling.

" you are so cute" he blushed at her compliment

In a few minutes, they were walking by the ocean. Such beauty and the people were doing well by keeping the place clean. There were fishermen around. Some were setting sail while some were returning, and some were preparing to set sail. Children were playing around as well. Teenagers going around with their friends and couples walking hand in hand

" beautiful isn't it ?" the young boy interrupted

" yes it is"

" what do you want to do here anyway?"

" Drown myself" she answered his question honestly. Looking down at the shocked and confused child she gave him this silly smile" see yeah" waved and with that, she left him alone

Lara continued walking, trying to get away from people because she knew if they found out she was trying to drown herself they would rescue her instantly.

Walking into the woods, she travelled past tall trees tripping severally due to the rocky environment, The melodies created by birds filled the wood. Lara climbed up to a cliff which she spotted some were in the woods. Perfect to dive into the water. As she got to the cliff top she was already panting due to how exhausted she was.

Standing at the edge of the cliff she look down at the water and damn it was terrifying. The force the water used to hit the rocks every second made her rethink her idea of jumping in but she wasn't ready to back out now, the sooner she got her memories, the sooner she would get out of this Island.

And just like that without thinking again, she jumped and it felt like her heart was about to leave her chest. The moment she crashed into the water, she didn't even get a chance to think as the water began to throw her from side to side. Struggled to swim so she wouldn't crash into a rock, only to realize that she had no idea how. She knew the lord wasn't on her side when the entire scene from the plane crash began to play in her head. Distracting her from everything. It felt like the plane crash was happening again. The whole memory played scattered in her head making it difficult for her to think straight, it felt so real. She struggled in the water for breath until she could no longer hold it again and accidentally took a breath." rrrr" Unbearable pain hit her as the water squeezed her brain burning her lungs. The water chucked the life out of her and damn, If only someone will come to her rescue right now. Just then a memory hit her

"I am leaving you. I can't take this any more, you are alone now. am sorry" A woman, whose face remained blurry spoke" *But I don't want to be alone mummy"* a child cried" *I want to go with you"*she cried bitterly," mummy please wait, don't go" her chest hurt even more as the memory played in her head. Who is this child? Is this my memory? She wonders, still in crisis

Suddenly, she felt strong arms around her waist and the next thing she knew she was out of the water, on the stand trying the get her breath back together, coughing in pain. She opened her eyes to meet the blurred environment.

The person helped her to sit up and began to tap her back as she coughed and coughed out water

" take it easy" A calm, familiar voice. He continued until she was settled. Lara looked up to meet those attractive ocean-blue eyes

" Malik ?" his name rolled out of her lips in a questioning manner trying to understand how he knew where she was

" are you alright ?" she could see all the worries in his eyes and feel it in his tone

" haa...yes. Happy to be alive. Once again thank you for saving me"

" Are you mad? why will you try to drown yourself?" he yelled taking her by surprise

" sorry I didn't mean to bother you"

" that doesn't answer the question. Do you want to die or what?" still yelling and this made her frown. Who does he think he is to yell at her

" don't you yell at me Malik" she scolded not expecting it to come out with so much authority

" Pardon?" shocked at her response

" I said don't yell at me" still sounding authoritative" if it wasn't for your crazy people I wouldn't be so desperate to get my memories back so I can get the hell out of here. Everyone believes that I am your future bride"

" oh," he grew a lot calmer than expected and had this guilty look. like a child who got caught stealing"then why drown yourselF"

" because Rebecca said that if I wanted to remember I have to go back to how it started, before I lost my memories. And it started at the plane crash"

" Rebecca told you to drown yourself?" he asked with a frowned

" She didn't say, Drown yourself. And besides it was a waste of time, such a big risk for nothing

" you didn't remember anything?" with a concerned look on his face.

" no I didn't" felling disappointed." but I saw something. A memory"

" what is it" he sat down in front of her with full interest, waiting for the story

" this woman." in deep thought looking at the sand to avoid eye contact" she said that she was leaving and there was this child that I think it's me. she cried for her not to leave"

" who is she?"

" her mother" she lifted her head to look him in the eyes" I think in my past, my mother left me and I cried, scared of being alone" There was silence between them for a short while.

"May she didn't leave, maybe she just went out" he said trying to sound positive

" No. she said she was sorry, she couldn't take it any more, she had to leave" Explained to Malik who now looked unhappy. Lara raised an eyebrow at him" Why do you look sad, it is my memory, not yours"

" Not just a memory but your past, you grew up without a mother"

" well I'm not the first, and besides it is just a single memory I don't know what really happened that made her want to leave."

" still. You grew up without a mother" She found myself smiling at him

" why do you care?"

" why won't I" he looked away and they were taken by silence once again. Her eyes fell on the ocean. Listening to the calming waves and enjoying the beauty of the water as the sun set on it. How can something this beautiful be this deadly?

Getting cold and needing warmth urgently. her eyes fell on Malik, also wet but didn't seem to be bothered by the cold" you want to get your memories back?" still looking away while he asked

" Yes. I need to"

" is it because you want to leave this island so that you won't have to marry me or because you just want it back" now looking at Lara

" and if I say it is because I want to leave so that I won't have to marry?" she answered with another question

" Just to get one thing clear. Do you hate me?"

" you saved my life twice now, I can't possibly hate you"

" well that is a start" sounding lively once again

" start to what?" curious to what he meant

" ignore that" he stood up" I think I know someone who can help. But first I have to get you back to the house, clean up and change into something warm" he offered his hand for her to take. Lara hesitated, staring at the hand. Why was she always terrified of being touched? She wonders deeply. Does this feeling have something to do with her past? But things are different now, these people saved her life so surely she is safe with them, isn't she? Especially the man in front of her, isn't he someone she should trust" oh sorry" apologizing immediately he remembers. About to take his hand away Lara took it

" no it's alright" says quickly" When a gentleman gives you a hand you shouldn't turn it down

" haa" a short laugh escaped his lips, looking down at the lady before him" ok" gently he helped her up" Let's go before you catch a cold" he spoke as calmly as ever.

C H A P T E R

6

The next morning as early as 7, the two left to find someone who could help. It was a long drive and a quiet one. Neither of them started a conversation, they just enjoyed the silence until

" so who are we going to see exactly?" She began, breaking the silence

"Doc Alex" he said with eyes focused on the road" She is a doctor and a psychologistic also a very close friend to the family

" so can she help me get my memories back" There was a sign of desperation in her tone.

" I don't know for sure, but I am certain she will have an idea of what to do" Lara nods in understanding" And I hope she does" he added

"me too"

" so now that you don't remember your name, we have to give you one"his eyes fell on her for a brief moment, then back on the road

" Guinevere" she responded

" Pardon?" an eyebrow raised

" Cordelia gave it to me"

" Guinevere" he repeats the name ," I like it. It suits you well." He smiles" white wave, she picked a good one, she always does"

" always ?"

" she is the best at giving names"

" oh" nodding" what does Cordelia mean then"

" Daughter of the sea" he looked at her while he spoke" You know, the family always tries to bear names that connect with the sea"

" I notice. What about yours?"

"King of the wave." sounding bold with eyes wide open, a sign of amazement

" yeah" giving a short smile

****

They arrived at Dr Alex's compound, the moment they stepped out of the car, A dog came running towards them. At first, she almost panicked but when Malik shouted its name" poff. Oh lord, I've missed" bent down letting the dog jump on him. She calmed down. The dog barked and wiggled its tail as Malik wrapped his arms around it, throwing different compliments at it.

" I see you remembered me today" a female voice interrupted. Lara lifted her head to see a plump woman standing at the cottage watching them, with her arms crossed. A beautiful woman with golden hair and around her late forties.

" Dr Alex?" Malik called. He carried the dog and led Lara towards the woman who didn't take her eyes off her

" and who is the beautiful maiden?" with a warm welcoming smile

" This is Guinevere" he introduced

" good morning" nervously

" morning" she walks down the steps." so you finally come to visit" she says to Malik as she walks past him to Lara. Before Lara could react, she was pulled in for a very strong hug. Lara just remained stiff in shock" how are you dear"

" I...I am... fine" still stiff and feeling awkward. Dr Alex pulls away and turns to Malik who puts down the dog wanting to hug her but she does something unexpected. Knocked Malik on the head. So hard that Lara could hear the sound it made

" Ouch" shouts in pain while rubbing his head" Why?"

" do you think I am getting any younger, why haven't you come to see me all this while." she scolded

" I have been busy with work" grumbling like a kid

" that is not an excuse" she said knocking his head again

" Ouch. Will you stop it!!!?" he yelled, then paused in shock realizing what he just did. Alex's eyes wide open in horror

" did you just yell at me?" she bent down to grab her slippers

" no, no, no, no" he began to run immediately Dr Alex followed him with her slippers ready to beat the hell out of him" I am sorry" cries out

" now you have grown wings haa" running after him and they faded into somewhere around the house. The young confused woman stood awkwardly alone. A few seconds later she giggled at the thought of Malik getting beaten up. The people of this island are dramatic, this was something she has noticed. Looking down at the dog who just stood in front of her, staring. She wanted to go down and pet it but didn't

After a long while of standing alone. Malik was walking back with his arms around Dr Alex, saying something that made her roll her eyes. They approached her. Dr Alex pushed Malik away and then took her hand" please forgive me for the awkward welcoming, this child needed a little discipline" she rolled her eyes at Malik who smiled at her childishly" and I failed to recognise who you were"

" Pardon?"

" Malik tells me you are his future wife" Her eyes fell on Malik in shock and he looked away like an idiot who knows what he did wrong

" it must be a mistake" giving an awkward smile

"Don't be silly darling. The matchmaker never makes a mistake. I thought the same for my husband but we turned out to be a happy couple. To sad he left so soon." sadness flashed in her eyes

" I am sorry" Lara bit her lower lips.

" don't be sorry, it has been three years now and besides I will always have him in here" She placed her hand on her chest while the sadness in her eyes slowly vanished" Now come on let's go inside"

All are seated in the sitting room. they were offered tea and for a doctor, Lara didn't expect her to add a lot of sugar to her tea and still say" *this is bitter*" Lara remained shocked at her words

Malik Explained the situation while Dr Alex listened with full attention. They were taken by silence when Malik finished. She thought for a long time. During this time, Lara's eyes explored the environment. It was a beautiful place, filled with nature. From the glass wall, she could see the backyard. She had a beautiful garden going on, a perfect place for one to relax. A tree somewhere in the middle of the garden with a bird cage swinging on one of its branches. It will be lovely to listen to the birds sing. The family picture frame on the wall had her, a man that she assumed was her husband and a young girl who was around her early twenties. And on the cabinet by the side was a smaller frame of her, the man and the girl when she was much younger.

" Have you tried anything yet" Dr Alex asked, calling her back to the matter at hand

" hammm. Yes I did" her eyes fell on Malik

" she drowned herself" Malik said with a frown and she could see the shock in Dr Alex's eyes when she heard Malik's words

" why?"

" I lost my memory after the plane crash and I thought that if I go back to how it started, I will remember something"

" And did you remember anything ?" leans forward in her chair

" no. nothing useful" Dr Alex nods and the went silence once again

" people tend to remember things when they do something that they are familiar with or love" she brocks the silent" like hobbies"

" I don't know if I have any hobbies"

" that means you will have to try different hobbies out there to find yours. You will definitely get something that will catch your attention something that when do it you will feel a sense of familiarity"

" ok" both nodding as they processed her words

" that means we are going to be busy for a while" Malik said

" We?" looking at him with a confused face

" yes we" he smiled.

He will help me? Lara thought. why will he help a woman who wants to leave him? Or possibly he also didn't want to marry her.

" wait here" Dr Alex stood up and walked away into one of the many rooms

" why are you helping me" she asked in whisper

" because helping you means me helping myself" he replies in his normal tone. She was glad that he didn't want to marry her as well

" glad that we are on the same page" he raised an eyebrow at her words. About to say something when Dr Alex walks in holding two small white containers. She hands them over to her

" hey. They are vitamins for memory loss. I am sure it will be of help"

" thank you" reaching out to them. The moment her hand touched the containers her head began to ache and a flash of a memory came to her

"*take this*" it was a male voice, and the environment was too bright so she couldn't see his face" *They are vitamins, it will help but it won't be of much help if you don't get good rest*" the man sounded worried and a hand-collected it, followed by a female voice

"*thank you*" the tone was a reluctant one and familiar

"*I am serious, you need rest, get a few days off work*"

"*I will keep that in mind*" it was certainly her memory. That means she has collected vitamins like this before but for what?

"Guinevere are you alright" she was called back to reality by that male voice. She opened my eyes to see Malik bent down in front of her with worries and concern on his face. Asked as he cupped her face into his larger palm" Guinevere what is wrong?"

" aaa" a gasp escaped her lips. She felt Dr Alex above her rubbing her back to calm her down

" does your head hurt? or anywhere?"

" no, I just remembered something"

" oh. You got us worried for a moment there" Dr Alex said. Lara noticed the relief on Malik's face and gave a soft smile

" thank goodness. Dropping his hand from her face to her hands. he cupped both of them and gave them a soft squeeze

" what did you remember?"

" nothing useful. Just that I was once given this kind of vitamin before"

" you were given these vitamins before?" Dr Alex had a curious tone" Why?"

" I don't know." she sighs" like I said nothing useful"

" We should get going, Malik announced as he tried to pull her up

****

The first 10 minutes of the drive was silent until she broke the silence" why did you tell Dr Alex that I am your future wife?" A silly smile made its way to his lips

" Because you are"

" Don't be ridiculous" rolled her eyes" I said the match maker made a mistake

" the matcher maker never makes mistakes" he spoke sounding confident

" I thought you also didn't want to marry me?"

" When did I say that ?" looks at her in confusion

" You said, you were helping me to help yourself."

" I am. Helping you to help myself. Getting to spend time with each other through the processes of helping you, who knows what will happen from there. And to be honest, I already had a thing for you before the matchmaker said anything"

" if that is the case then don't help me" she frowned. So this was his plan, all along.

" that means you will be stuck here with no memory and eventually marry me" he shrugs

" you are such an idiot"she snapped at him

" Ouch" with his left hand on his chest, he cried dramatically

"This is no joke" angrily. he gave her that usual warm smile but when he noticed she was almost on edge, he adjusted

" alright." suddenly becoming serious" Look, I will not lie. I do like you and I don't know why, I just like you. But I will not force marriage on you. it also doesn't make sense to me. I mean if I ended up somewhere with no memory and I am suddenly asked to marry a stranger I will be swimming that ocean by now trying to get out at all cost" she suddenly giggled.

" that is too dramatic"

" Dramatic, but true. I won't be worrying about shakes or anything, just as long as I get out of here." he shrugs while the young lady laughs. For the first time in the few days of knowing Lara, she laughed and it sounded just amazing" look, I do want to help because it is the right thing to do and ALSO" he emphasized on the also" we will get to know each other in the process, maybe you will get to see that I deserve to be given a chance" She smiled at him trying to hold back more laughter

" you are a nice guy but it is still not happening" he gave a cute disappointed smile

" I can't give up yet, we only just started"

****

They drove into town and surprisingly Malik stopped in front of a fish shop" why are we here" he killed the engine.

" We left this afternoon without eating so..."

" You want to eat fish?"

" grilled fish" he announced." Mr Tomas makes the best grilled fish in town and not only is it delicious it is also appealing to the eyes and the seasoning is just right"

" ok....."

" If you are going to be on this island for a while you have to try out the best things we have. You should try his catfish first"

" sure. Whatever you say" shrugs reluctantly

The two got out of the car and made their way to the shop. A container shop with an open-up sales window, the smell of fish filled the air but a pleasant one" Malik" an old man who was busy smoking his fish called out with excitement at the sight of the both of them

" Mr Tomas" now standing in front the shop with a bright smile" oh Lord I've missed your fish"

" Always the fish and not me" he frowned

" oh come on you know I miss you too. Without you who will make me my favourite dish ?"

" This boy" he wiggled his spatula to Malik's face in a warning

" oh Mr Tomas" laughed

" And this must be our future lady" his eyes fell on Lara and he grinned

" oh yes. Meet Lady Guinevere" Lara rolls her eyes at Malik

" hi" was all she said

" you are as beautiful as they speak"

" Thank you" giving a small smile that faded as quickly as it came

" so I have brought her here to try out your amazing dish. One of the island's very best"

" oh really" overwhelmed" Have a seat and in a few minutes I will make you two something special" he says. Malik helped Lara to bring a stool over and she sat down while he sat next to her" I am almost done with this, A customer is coming over to pick it up" he informed pointing to the previous one he was working on

" oh, no problem" Malik said then turned to Lara

" you are going to love this"

" I can't wait" being sarcastic

" but anyways. About your memories. Do you have anything in mind you want to try out"

" no"

" then I have to come up with something" with that he went into a deep thought.

Mr Tomas finished with the previous one and in about 40 minutes he was done with theirs. A whole fish on a small tray well prepared and indeed appealing to the eyes

" wow. This does look good"

" try it" Mr Tomas offered her a fork and bowed like she was a queen. This put a bright smile on her face as she collected the fork

" Thank you" they watched in silence as she cut out a piece from it and ate. She chewed slowly at first, but in a little while her chewing grew faster" this is good" eyes wide open

" yes" the two men shout in union and give themselves high-fives

" I told" Malik spoke proudly

" oh God" enjoying the dish

" Give me my fork" he instructed Mr Tomas who went in to grab him a fork

The two had small comfortable conversations while they ate. Mr Tomas was quite entertaining with his customers and in the end, Lara promised to return for another dish

Malik stopped in front of a building that said" *Millie's Best Dance Club"* which was a bit weirder than when they stopped in front of a fish shop

" what are we doing here?" looking at the building from the car window

" Dancing is a hobby, I figured we should start from here" he says. Lara turns to him with an eyebrow raised" and it is also fun"

" surely dancing is not my thing"

" We will find out" he got out of the car and she rolled my eyes at him

****

The sun was already going down as they drove back to the house, laughing and mocking her ridiculous dance moves" I told you it was not my thing"

" I thought that maybe it is because you don't remember, that is why you say it is not your thing and besides everyone should be able to do some moves" his laughter filled the air

" well my case it is different"

" yeah it is" he said trying to hold a little of his laugh but couldn't

" stop it"

" sorry but it is just too funny" Looking at him, she as well couldn't hold herself back and had to join in. They were taken by silence not long.

Looking out the car window, she rested her arm on the window. Watching as the trees kept falling behind them like a wind. she closed her eyes and inhaled deeply enjoying the breeze. Suddenly the breeze grew stronger, she opened her eyes to notice that Malik had opened the roof of the car. He smiled at her and then focused on the road once again. There was this feeling of freedom inside of her as the breeze hit her skin and messed up her hair.

" you should smile more often" he breaks the comfortable silence

" Pardon ?" totally confused at his words

" smile more often, most of the time you carry a straight face. No emotion"

"When you say most times it sounds like you have known me long." she gave him this look that said. Really?

" no, I haven't but I remember the first time we met, when you entered the kitchen. You had the straight face that honestly frightened me a little and then you were like ' *hi*'" he looks at her with a grin" and to be honest you looked kind of cute"

"Really?"

" yes. And most of the time your smile is fake. Many may not notice but I do"

" I see" reluctantly looking away

"And also you look very pretty when you do"sounding more calm and deep. Looking back at him. Not expecting him to say those words

" well I will keep that in mind" this time sounding less reluctant

In a few minutes, they were driving towards his mansion. He stopped in front and they both got out. Just as he was getting out, he got a call. Lara began walking, leaving him to take the call. she was about to put in the door password he called her name" Guinevere ?"

" yes" turns around to see him still standing next to the car

" I have to head to the lab something came up"

" oh" nodded in understanding, wondering why he was telling her before leaving. Was he asking for permission or something?

" get a good rest. When I get back we will go somewhere"

" where ?"

" to see my family" he said, about to to get into the car

" what... why ?" stopped him midway

" my mother wants to see her future in law"

" but we are not getting married" she reminded just in case he had forgotten

" well the family doesn't know that, and I am sure you don't want to make an old lady cry" With that he gave her that sweet smile, got into the car and drove off leaving her in total lost.

" I really have to leave this island" whispered.

CHAPTER

7

8 PM, when they left for Malik's Family mansion. With no idea what to wear to her future husband's family house. She just dressed in the usual trousers and T-shirt just as long as she looked decent. Looking out the car window she watched the trees fall behind and enjoyed the breeze as it hit her skin and messed up her hair

" worried?" Malik suddenly asked

" pardon"

" Are you worried that they won't like you"

" why would I?"

" Usually, when daughters in law go to see the family, they get worried that the family won't like them"

" I will be grateful if they don't" she said. At that moment, like she spotted a sign of disappointment on his face but she didn't care" It will make it easier to get out of here"

" Indeed it would"

They didn't say anything to each other until they arrived at the mansion.

As they drove in. The feeling she got was just like the one from the other night of the festival. the feeling of amazement and excitement. Perfect, is what the place is to be called, the way nature filled the environment made it so beautiful.

" I don't think I will ever get used to this" she spoke as Malik parked in front of the house

" used to what ?" curiously

"This view" they got out of the car, her eyes explored. She watched as that young man from the other night came to take the car key from Malik, got in and drove off.

" you would but you won't get bored of it" replied from behind me. she turned to look at him, to see that he had put his hand out for her to take making her raise an eyebrow" look, my family doesn't know that you don't want to marry me and I would like to keep it that way. Making them unhappy is the least of my priorities"

" but they will find out eventually, what difference will it make?"

" by then I would have come up with something but for now." he hesitates" Please help me put a smile on their faces"he says with that low calm tone which made it difficult to say no

" OK"

" thank you" smiles brightly waiting for her to take his hand which she did.

Malik led her into the mansion. Past the empty hall, he led her to the sitting room and they spotted Cordelia and Rebecca chatting

" Good evening" Malik greeted with a smile, calling the both of them attention

" Guinevere" Cordelia called with excitement and she hurried to come to embrace Lara" I didn't believe that you would actually come. How did you convince her" looks at Malik who shrugs

" where is mother ?" changing the question

" in the kitchen preparing dinner. She refuses to let the cook do it saying she wants to cook specially for her future daughter-in-law

" Mother I'm home" Malik calls and there is no respond

" Aunt, your daughter-in-law is here" Cordelia announced and immediately they heard something fall and a door open" And here she comes" in a mocking tone.

In a short while Malik's mother walked into the sitting room heading straight for Lara, with excitement written all over her face

" oh my God"eyes on Lara

" Hohandara mama" she pushed Malik out of the way, ignoring his greeting and pulled Lara for a strong warm hug" oh sweat heart" from across her shoulder Lara saw the shocked Malik, due to his mother's action. Feeling stiff and not knowing how to react. This island deals with too much body contact which will take a while for Lara to get used to.

" ok, ok Mother time out" Malik cuts in immediately he notices her discomfort" she needs space and rest, we have been out all day" gently pulling his mother away from her

" you.." she gave Malik a heavy knock on the head" Let me hold my daughter-in-law. Go away"

" ouch, ouch" robbing his head" mother why"

" get out" she scolds and turns back to Lara

" nice to meet you too ma" feeling awkward. The woman studied her from head to toe and flashed a smile. She could see where Malik gets his smile, his everything.

" and she is such a black beauty" she complimented as she looked at Malik and then back at the young lady in front of her

" thank you. And you are also very beautiful ma"

" oh come on" she blushes using her hands to cover her face" I am old now, it is all fading" putting her hands back down.

" no it is not, honesty you are very beautiful, that was what came to my mind when I first saw you"

" oh my God" her face turned as red as a tomato making her look cute" I like her" nodding to Malik" Come on dear" She grabbed Lara's hand like they were a couple leading her to the couch. Lara smiled at Rebecca who she only just remembered was also present in the room and Rebecca smiled back in response" come sit close to me." she did as the woman said" Now, tell me about you ?" Lara looks at her in confusion, then at Malik not knowing how to answer. and just like a superhero Malik suddenly sits close to his mother on the other side

" you see Mother" he began with a serious tone but calm" Guinevere doesn't remember her past" Lara was in shock. She did not expect him to be so honest with his mother like that.

" what do you mean" the woman sounded worried

" Remember that plane crash I told you about and the woman I saved" She nods" She is that woman" his mother was taken by surprise

" so you don't know who you are? how are you going to marry my son with no memory?"

"Mother don't worry about that" he says calling her attention" We are working on getting her memories back and we already met with Dr Alex.... She told us what to do" his mother didn't look pleased at all" Mother don't worry. You know this will be an opportunity for the both of us to get to know each other and also" he smiles and whispered something to his mother's ear which made her smile as well

" I see" nodding

"And I like her" he announced with a gentle gaze on her. His eyes were telling her something she couldn't read. For a moment she thought she felt something, something in her chest" I don't know her well but there is something about her that calls my attention" his mother gives him another heavy knock

" don't make her feel uncomfortable on her first visit"

" ouch" cries in pain

" so darling, tell me, what do you think about my son" Lara stares at Malik remembering that he pleaded for her to help put a smile on his family's face

" I like him. He seems like a sweet guy"

" He is a sweet guy" praising her son" what is do you like about him"

" ammmm" thinks" I don't know" sounding nervous with her honesty

" True love is not knowing why you like someone but you do." Lara grins awkwardly

" if you say so ma"

" don't call me that, call me mother" completely taken aback. did she really mean that? did she just tell a total stranger to call her mother? From what Lara remembers her mother had left her for reasons she knows not of. But here she was, someone else wants her to call her mother

" do you truly mean that?"

" yes, darling. I am your mother from now on, I know you have your own mother but it doesn't matter. It is not wrong to have two mothers." the overwhelming joy that took over her was unexplainable, but she remained as calm as ever, showing nothing but a simple smile.

" OK"

" Aunt Thalassa you never told me to call you mother and I am also like a daughter to you" Rebecca suddenly interrupts

" yes you are but Guinevere right here is my future daughter In law, there is a deference" Rebecca rolled her eyes in a joking manner

" you don't even know her the way you know me"

" I don't but I will. And besides you will leave us eventually to find your own mate but she is with us for life" used her hand to cup Lara's face like she was a little child" you are so pretty my dare"

" if you keep saying that then what will I say about you? I saw how beautiful you were the other night and now that I sit before you, I am totally speechless"

" auwwww. That is so sweet" blushing" ok I will leave you and Malik alone" stood up" I have to go finish preparing dinner. I know you two have a lot of catching up to do,"

" What about father?" Malik asked, stopping her from leaving

" he had a meeting with the elders. Will be back soon"

" Oh, ok" with that Lady Thalassa left the sitting room. And silence lived among them for a short while before Rebecca broke it.

" Malik, can we talk alone for a moment?" sounding odd

" sure" they also left the room

****

Malik and Rebecca returned a while later, Looking like they had a serious fight

" what happened with you two" Cordelia asked with an eyebrow raised" it looks like you two just had a fight" she mocked

" I am leaving" Rebecca announced

" so soon, I thought you wanted to spend the night" Cordelia was disappointed

" Well someone out of nowhere already took my spot" Rebecca's eyes landed on Lara as she spoke angrily while the innocent lady wondered what she did wrong that got her angry

" Rebecca don't make me do something that you will hate me for" Malik scolded surprising everyone. Her eyes fell wide open in confusion and shock to see Malik speak that way. What did the two talk about that got them acting strange? What did Rebecca say to him?

" I will take my leave now" She rolled her eyes and they watched in silence as the angry young lady walked out of the house, closing the door behind her.

****

Rebecca

Rebecca closed the door behind her angrily. Walking down the stairs she tries to hold back her tears. All her hard work, all her effort of trying to get close to the fishers, just so she could be with Malik is put to drain in just a few days by some lady who didn't even put any effort. Damn that matchmaker for her visions, damn this entire island.

She walked to where her car was parked, opened it and got in. closing both windows and doors, making sure no one heard her and then." fuccccck!!!!!!!" she screamed still trying to hold back her tears" aaaaaaaaaaaaaaaaaaaaaa" breathing heavily. Rebecca flashed back to when they were still kids when she first met Malik. It was love at first sight. She flashed back to how she always followed Malik around no matter what. How Malik helped her when she needed help and how she always tried to stand up for him when he was in trouble. Rebecca has always done her best to be around Malik, to be part of his life. She did her best to even study the same course as he did so they would work together at the lab. Even if she knew very well that Malik never liked her that way. She had always hoped that maybe, just maybe he would finally realize what she meant to him" who is this girl anyway" whispers under her breath, In deep thought. Rebecca reached for her phone in her pocket and then dialled a number" hello" she said the moment the call was answered" it's been a long time indeed" smiled" I want you to help me find out about someone," her smile dropped" I will send you a picture tomorrow"

CHAPTER

8

Dinner with the fishers turned out much better than expected, the family were amazing to be with. Lara got to meet Malik's sister, Anahita, who just returned from boarding school in Canada along with three of her friends who came to visit the island. Mr Ford, Malik's father was surprisingly very nice and carefree and he also gave bad dad jokes which made the room laugh endlessly

" so in a few years or even months I will be having grandchildren running around in this house" he suddenly created an awkward silence, making the innocent young girl's food stop somewhere around her chest and begin coughing. Malik immediately came to her aid, handing her a glass of water while he rubbed her back

" Father why did you suddenly have to make her uncomfortable" Anahita spoke out in defence

" it was just a question"

" surely you will have grandchildren Father it is not something you have to ask and very beautiful ones for that matter" The little girl wiggled her eyebrow at Lara, instantly Lady Thalassa threw a spoon at her which she dodged

" you stupid girl"

" no throwing things at the table" Anahita says to her mother in a joking manner

" are you talking to me like that?" looking and sounding dramatic

" mother it is your words not mine" she lifts her hand in surrender

" so you are using my words against me now" still being dramatic

" o come on mother" Malik sat down and wrapped his arms around his mother

" she is speaking the truth"

" so you are supporting her" she woman grabs his ear

" aya, aya, aya" struggling in pain with his eyes closed

" Mother how can you do that in front of his bride? It is embarrassing" Anahita said

" you...." Mr Ford cut her off

" I agree don't you see his bride is watching" she supported

" I see you are all against me ha....." nodding in disbelieve as she looked around" You" She let Malik go as her eyes fell on her husband" I will deal with you later" Her words had a serious effect on him, he gave an apologetic look then says to Anahita

" hey..... apologize to your mother"

Lara smiled while watching the family entertain her and had fun at the dining table. She began to wonder how her family were in her past life. Did she get to talk, laugh and argue at the dining table just like this? If her mother left, what about her father? How was her relationship with her father?

Time for the girls to go to sleep. Anahita pulled Lara along with her and her friends to the bedroom. While Lara wondered what they wanted with her.

She watched them get into bed quickly. Then Anahita asked her to sit on the bed next to her which she did" tell us a story" the girl said

" Pardon ?" looking at the kids with confusion written on her face

" tell us a story. You have to know how to tell stories if you are going to be a member of this family

" but I don't know any stories"

" that is not possible" she frowned" how can you not have any story"

" I agree" her friend lying right next to her supported

" so if I can't tell stories I will not be accepted into the family" asked with amazement in her tone and the girl shrugged

" that is bulshit" That familiar voice suddenly interrupted calling everyone's attention. They turned to the direction of the voice to see Malik at the door side. When did he come? They had no idea. Or how long he has been standing there

" what are you? a police officer or something" he frowns

" well, I have to approve of the woman that marries my brother"

" go to bed, no story for you tonight" walking forward

" That is not fair" the three girls said looking disappointed

" sometimes life isn't fair"

" wait" cutting the siblings off" I think I can come up with something"

" yes," the girls said in unison. Anahita stuck out her tongue to her brother and Malik did the same, while Lara held back a laugh

" ok let's do this" they adjusted themselves waiting for her to speak

" ok I want you all to imagine this as we go okay" They nodded in response and from the corner of her eyes, she saw Malik sit down in a chair at the reading table

"once upon a time. Deep in the forest, there was this boy
who lived in a cave alone with his mother"
" give me a name" Lara said to the girls

" Adam" one said excitedly

" ok" nodding and went back to the story

" his name is Adam. Never even once has Adam seen the
outside world. All he sees is light from a distance but
never does he goes outside. He waits in the cave for his
mother to return home with food and clothes and any
time he asks his mother why he can't go outside,
she replies" that the world out there is very cruel and
evil. I must protect you from the world". She says. She
does this because of the motherly love she has for him and
Adam will smile knowing that his mother loves him so much
and only wants to protect him. But one day when his mother
doesn't return home early, Adam's curiosity gets the best of
him and he sets out to go outside even if it is only for a
minute. The moment Adam stepped out, he was overwhelmed
with the beauty of the outside world, the warmth of the
sun as it hit his skin, the wind, the beautiful blue sky
and the feeling of the grass beneath his feet. It was perfect. nothing
like inside the cave which was cold and empty and dark
Adam wanted to go inside but decided to take another step
and another, and a few more on till Adam found himself
wondering the forest lost. He tried to find his way back
home but it was pointless. Suddenly it began to rain and
Adam runs for shelter.

She told them the entire story and to her surprise they listened with full interest. There was this feeling she had while she spoke. The feeling of familiarity that Dr Alex spoke of. Is this her hobby or something?" that was a sad story" one of Anahita's friends said sounding disappointed

" yes it was" Anahita supported

" well in life there is never truly a happy ending" smiles" you don't like it?"

"We do" they spoke in Union sadly.

" but I would have preferred it if he became prince, not die" one of them said

" that witch is so evil. First, she pretends to be his mother and locks him in a cave then comes back to kill him. All for what? Because his father offended her? That is so not fair, why blame the innocent boy for his father's mistake" Anahita grumbled

" life is not fair sometimes. Good and innocent people suffer the most and sometimes do not get anything in the end"

" that is not nice" Anahita obviously wasn't pleased with the ending

" ok time for bed" Malik stood up and walked towards them

" will you tell us another tomorrow ?" She gave puppy eyes, Malik rolled his eyes at his sister. He pulls Lara up to a standing position

" good night Ana. Lara needs rest" he says

Memory

" the ending. we have talked about this over and over again. Your work is great but the ending is always a problem. Fans are beginning to complain"
" there is nothing wrong with the ending"
" The script is not going to sell"
****

Davina

"OK love, see you tonight"were her final words before ending the call. Davina Throws her phone on the couch while rolling her eyes" I have to put an end to this relationship as soon as possible" the thought of the person she just spoke to got her irritated. Grabs the TV remote, switching to different channels on till something catches her attention.

".......found a body in the ocean" the reporter spoke from the scene, instantly Davina's heart skipped" It turns out to be the body of the flight attendant who was also in the plane before the plane crash. But there is still no sign of our Dear Director write, Omolara Tosin. The public is beginning to suspect that she is dead and her body was shattered in the crash. But the police will not back down until there is proof. Will Omolara Tosin be found dead or alive ?"

" Damn the fucking police" she yells throwing the remote at the TV" Can't they just let it go" frowns then the thought of the industry came to her" It looks like I'll have to pay someone a visit"

****

Davina confidently walks into Mr James' office taking him by surprise. Never in his wildest imagination did he think he would ever see Davina in his office after the last incidence

" Davina ?" he stood up from his chair, she could sense the shock in his voice which put a smile across her lips

" Mr James. Why? you don't look pleased to see me." taking a few steps closer to the table

" what are you doing here?"

" you know" she shrugs and takes a seat" have you been able to reach Lara yet" her question got him confused

" is that even a question or are you not aware of what is going on" frowns

" I am, and I am also aware that you are waiting for her return. Not to forget that everyone is waiting for her new movie"

" I have a feeling you know her where about"

" oh" she gives a pitiful face" And if I do?" grins" You think I'm gonna tell...... I do not give a shit about Lara's whereabouts

" then why are you here?"

" I am here because my offer still stands."

" I told you to give it up" James says angrily

" oh don't be like that. Lara is nowhere to be found, the industry will fall if you don't do something about the situation and besides people are already complaining about her stories don't you think it is time for some adjustment"

" I have hundreds of writers in this industry and why will I use you?"

" because I used to be the best among those writers and now that Lara is out of the picture I am still the best" There was silence between them for a long while. Mr James finally sits down with interest. He leans forward placing both arms on the table, with fingers locked to each other.

" What is in for you?" asked and Davina smiled leaning forward knowing that they were now talking business

" I want it all back, my position, my status, everything"

" you killed your statues with your own hands remember?" the smile on her face instantly faded" You accused Lara of infringement when you were the one who copied her works"

" well, that is in the past. No one remembers that"

" Have you googled your name? That is the first thing that comes up"

" no one will remember that when we give them something else to talk about. And I have just what it is, what the people want" Mr James thinks for a while,

Always on the side that brings him a profit, he is a businessman after all" I give you a splendid story, you give me back my power. What do you say" he grins

" if you can keep to your word then you got yourself a deal" they both shack hands

" wow Mr James, just a few minutes ago it seemed like you were dead loyal to Lara and now?"

" what can I say, it is just business" They both smiled at each other

****

Rebecca

"what is wrong with you, it has been two weeks and still nothing" Rebecca who had been doing research on Lara, scolded someone on the phone. She was getting really pissed off with their lack of progress

" ma please give us time. All we have of this person is just a picture, it is taking longer than expected

" then what do I pay you for" she yells" Stop giving me excuses and give me results" She ends the call and just as she turns around she is met with the person she least expected." Guinevere!" her heart almost stopped functioning. At that moment she thought it was over for her, Guinevere already figured out what she was doing

" trouble from work?" Guinevere asked, confusing her.

" What ?"

" I meant at the lab. Malik told me that one of the mama whales and her baby went missing"

" oh, yeah." she nods" yes, still haven't found her" sighs in relief.

" sorry about that"

" nothing to worry about, by the way, what are you doing outside" she forced a smile" looking for something ?"

" looking for Malik actually" Lara replies while looking around to get any sight of him" he told me to meet him outside" The thought of Malik and Lara seeing each other alone outside made Rebecca so uncomfortable

" why? Are you two going out?"

" I don't know" Lara shrugs" he just told me to see him outside

" Guinevere" Rebecca takes a few steps forward. She stands in front of her with eyes locked on hers" I want to ask something"

" you don't have to stand too close" She takes a few steps back

" if you finally get your memories back" she hesitates" Will you leave this island? leave Malik?" Lara didn't expect a question like that out of nowhere." will you leave ?" Rebecca asked more eagerly this time making her uncomfortable

" why will you ask her that?" that familiar voice suddenly spoke from behind Rebecca and he sounded very angry. Lara looks across Rebecca's shoulder while Rebecca turns around to see Malik, standing there, pissed off.

" Malik ?" the name rolled out of Rebecca's mouth weakly. She never thought he would be standing there.

" does her presence bother you?" asked

" no, you got me wrong. I just wanted to know what she does next after she gets her memories back"

" That should be her problem, not yours" scold

" Malik it is not something to be upset about, she just asked a question that is all" his eyes fell on Lara and they were all taken by silence for a while

" lets go" breaking the silence

" where are we going" Lara asked curiously

" where I work"

" you are taking her to the lab?" Rebecca's eyes fell wide open" You can't just let anyone into the lab"

" she is not just anyone" Malik says and puts out his hands for Lara to take. She was confused, wondering what was going on between Malik and Rebecca. She remembered Cordelia once told her that they were childhood friends and when she asked Cordelia what was happening between the two. She always says not to mind them" come, let's go" she walks up to Malik and takes his hand, giving Rebecca one final look before they walk away. While Rebecca stood there holding back her tears. The longer this woman stays on this island the more difficult it is to tolerate everything.

CHAPTER

9

Lara

"What are we going to do at the lab?" breaking the long silence in the car.

" there is a lot for you to see." he smiled" I want to you show the world under the ocean. Don't you want to see it?"

" I do" smiled back

" you will love it" he says before going quiet again. She stares at him for a while, wanting to hold back the question she wanted to ask

"Are you and Rebecca having issues because of me" finally threw the question at him. He looks at her with a frown

" what makes you say that?"

" I don't know" she shrugs" I just felt that way and usually I will ignore things like this but." stops to think" I have spent over two weeks on this island and I barely see or hear people have misunderstanding. if there is any, the chief and Lady Thalassa attend to it immediately. I think something I am beginning to love about this island is the way everyone relates"

" then what makes you think that it is because of you? Did Rebecca say something to you" with eyes focused on the road, The atmosphere around him changed

" I am not blind Malik, she didn't say anything. Cordelia once told me that you two are childhood friends. Why now when I am around?" he looks at her, and instantly his eyes soften as he notices her worries, then back at the road with this smile she's also beginning to love

" don't worry about it. We are like this sometimes" he says sounding like everything was a joke

" ok" gave a slight nod" if you say so"

****

" here we are" Malik announced as they arrived at a strange place. It was supposed to be a cave but it had a gate, a silver gate and there were three other cars packed outside. She looked at him with an eyebrow raised

" I thought....." not knowing how to phrase the question but he understood anyway.

" how do you think we go down there" he smiles while getting out of the car. He takes her hand and leads her to the gate. she watched him quietly put in the code and the gate opened. The inside looked like a tunnel, a bright tunnel with cameras. It grew colder as he led her through until they got to the elevator. There was a long silence between them as they went down but a comfortable one. She caught Malik staring at her one or two times and she knew he wanted to say something but didn't know how to start.

" If you have something to say just say it" turns to face him and gazes met

" you haven't said anything about your memories lately" he said

" that is because I haven't had anything meaningful. They are all scattered with no meaning"

" oh" he nods in understanding without taking his eyes off her, waiting for her to say more

" but"she began." There is this feeling I have been having but chose to ignore because I felt that it won't be of any help

" What is it?"

" Whenever I tell the kids stories I get this feeling" he raised an eyebrow" The feeling of familiarity that Dr Alex spoke of"

" why haven't you told me"

" it is useless. How can telling stories to help me"

" it can if it has something to do with your past"

" I think I was a" Just then the elevator door opened, and she instantly got distracted by the beauty of the place" Oh my god" the words rolled out of her lips while stepping out. The place was made of glass so the entire ocean was visible and it felt like she was under the ocean, well they were literally under the ocean and there was indeed a lot to see. She goes closer to the glass watching as the fishes swim by and along with other creatures." it's safe right" looked at Malik who kept smiling at her from behind

" yes, it is" found herself placing her hand on the glass and damn it was cold. she watched the underwater world with amazement in her eyes.

" so you work here?" impressed. She looked at him and then back at the ocean. Began walking fast, whirling from one spot to another like a crazy person

" yes"

" don't you get scared?"

" nope," There was a lot to see. A lot that can put a smile on anyone's face. Especially hers

" what if the glass breaks?"

" We won't let that happen"

" don't shakes come around?"

" They do" Her eyes fell wide open, turns to him

" they do? don't you get scared? What if it breaks the glass with its teeth what will happen then?" knowing Lara this was the first time she acted like a little kid and she looked so adorable, it made his heart swell. He bits his lower lips, holding back his laughter

" We won't let that happen"

" what are you feeling" crossing her arms" Some kind of animal hero" she mocked. Malik took a few steps closer to her, gently taking her hand

" it is my job to protect the ocean creatures. That means I will make sure violent creatures behave. Because if the ocean is safe then the island is safe" Malik looked in her eyes as he spoke and at that moment he looked cooler than ever, like a leader. The island is lucky to have such a wonderful chief. Lara thought to herself

" hearing you speak like that just made my heart flutter"

" Really?" proud" does that mea...." she cut him off

" you and I won't work" said and began walking away with a teasing smile. she heard his footsteps get louder and just like that he took her hand and began walking faster

" I want to show you something" pulling her along with him

" what?"

" my favourite creature of the ocean"

they stopped in front of the glass watching the fishes

" They are just fishes" looks at him with confusion written all over her face

" Just wait"

" OK...." rolls her eyes. She stood next to Malik looking deep into the dark ocean wondering what he wanted to show her. Lara was suddenly taken by surprise by something that covered the glass making her take a step back in panic" oh my God" breathing heavily. Malik caught her and pulled her gently to him, He rested her back on his chest with his hands on both her shoulders so she would relax. She finally saw it. A whale and a big one and there were three others along with that" whales" whispers. Amazed by the beauty of the creatures

" yeah," he responded with eyes on them. The calming sound of the whale filled the air. A perfect ocean melody

" what is it doing?"

" that is a male humpback" he points to the whale which makes the sound and she listens as the others respond in the same sound" They are communicating" he informs.

" is this why you like them"

" no" responded quickly not taking his eyes away from them" Their love for family is what I like about them. They love to be together, family is something that they treasure. Both sons and daughters remain with their mother throughout their lives." he says calmly and her attention is taken away from them to him" and the children's safety is the mother's first priority"

" A lot like this island's people"

" yeah it is" dropping his head to look down at her" they always remind me of home"

" I wish I had a home like that." sadly" from what I remember my mother left and I have no idea why and I don't remember a thing about my father. I wonder what our relationship had been like"

" you have a family now" his words instantly left her speechless. Their gaze met

" Pardon?" in a low tone. He stares deep into her softly. Lara felt completely naked in his eyes. Staring into her soul trying to tell her something she didn't quite understand." what is it?" almost finding it hard to voice out

" never mind me" he puts an end to the topic" I wanted to ask you something"

" about what"

" the stories you tell my sister" Lara moved away from him so she would be able to turn around and face him" I notice they all end sadly why ?"

" Can I ask you something first?"

" sure"

" do you believe that there is truly a happy ending?" Malik found the question deep, she noticed from the look he gave. She watches him think for a while

" yes"

" well, I do not." ending with the girl of your dreams is not a happy ending. Becoming successful is not a happy ending. Love is not a happy ending"

" you sound like you were one heartbroken"

" I won't know. I can't remember" she reminded" what I am trying to say is that. Once you think that you finally have a happy ending you find out that there is a whole messed-up series that follows. That is when life becomes more difficult and messed up" Malik smiled at her" why are you smiling?"

" I like the fact that you are a realist" he says

" I appreciate the compliment"

" And I agree with you there, when you said that a Happy ending doesn't mean having the girl of your dreams or love or being successful" his eyes were now focused on the whales" You want to know what a happy ending is to me?"

" what?"

" It is what happens during the messed up series that follows"

" Now you got me lost"

" finding love will not be a happy ending unless it is proven that, that love is strong enough. Yes, things may happen, no money, problems with not having children and other family problems and so many things. But the ability for the two to remain together during those times, fighting all odds is what makes it a happy ending. The same goes with a successful man. Definitely, there will be ups and downs in his business, completion. But is he strong enough to carry on? does he have people he trusts around him? Competent workers? And most of all is he happy?" he looked down at her now and their gaze met" That is a happy ending to me. do you understand"

" yes." nodded in understanding. She has never thought of it that way" what do you think your happy ending will be, Malik"

" you" replies quickly

" What ?" shock not expecting the respond

" I want you to stay Guinevere" words that got her speechless for a moment" I want you to stay on the island with us, with me" and her heart fluttered

"Malik we...." he cut her off

" I know. you don't have to tell me again" She saw signs of sadness in his eyes and she wondered why. She thought they settled this at the beginning

They were interrupted by whale sounds that got Malik's attention immediately" I know that sound" he looked away from her to the ocean. she watched him search through other fishes and whales and they both saw it. A much smaller whale heading towards the glass" Teresa" he called the name with excitement in his tone

" Who?" looking at him confused

" Teresa" the baby whale that went missing he sounded so excited" o my god" his phone rang and he took the call

" sir are you seeing this" the person said from the other end sounding excited as well

" yes, I am. What about her mama"

" We are still on the search"

" alright I am heading there now" Malik said and ended the call. she saw the joy in those eyes which looked sad just a few seconds ago. It isn't a good sight when Malik isn't happy. She thinks to herself" let's go"

" where?"

" where I actually work" he took her hand and began leading her deep into the lab and she followed not holding back the joy of seeing Malik so happy.

****

As early as 6 am she hears knocking on her door. Lara goes to open it and sees Malik standing there all dressed for the day." arr Malik. What is it" a sleepy tone

" it is time to wake up"

" Do you want die to day" frowns

" that is a bit cold" Dramatically scared

" what do you want ?"

" freshen up, we are going to the library"

" Library?"

" yes. If you get a feeling of familiarity when telling the kids stories then it has something to do with books. What do you think?"

" that is quite true" sleepy, she nods

"Now get dressed. I will be waiting for you downstairs" sounding energetic

" I hate you Malik" frowning

" and I love you" wiggling his eyebrow. Lara rolls her eyes at him and slams the door at his face" hurry up. You don't have to look prettier than you already do" he yells from outside

Miya Kwen

CHAPTER

10

L ady Thalassa had taken Lara to town to speak with the people of the island. To know how they were doing, and if they had any issues that should be brought down to the chief and so on. It is one of the most important responsibilities of the Lady of the island. They also ran a few language lessons, to improve her understanding of their language.

Lara sat on her bed completely exhausted from such a long day. She fell back, spreading both hands on the bed with her eyes closed. Inhales deeply. Suddenly, she flashed back to that night" *I want you to stay, stay with me*" that word made her heart flutter and still does." Guinevere get yourself together. The plan is to get your memory and get out of here, even if it is taking longer than planned" scolding herself. She is then interrupted by a knock on the door" who is it?"

" Malik" his voice made her heart skip" may I come in?"

" oh, yes" she stood up as he opened the door. She hasn't seen him in a while due to his busy schedule. Rebecca had told her something about a very important business. Now that he stood in front of her, she only just realized how much she missed him.

" Good evening" He greeted

" evening"

" how have you been?"

" good and busy" She shrugs

" I'm aware. You know if you don't like it you should just say so, mother won't force you" he steps forward

" to be honest, I do enjoy it. Especially going to see Imran's family" she laughed, something she does more often lately and had no idea how Malik loved to hear it. It was like a wonderful melody in his ear

" That kid is something else" joining in the laughter

" honestly" she sat down on the bed" You know, today he told his mother that he will be supper rich and buy her an aeroplane" She began to narrate what happened during their encounter

" or really, that is so sweet of him" Malik, impressed by the boy's words

" I'm not done yet" holding back her laugh" so his mother told him that he can't be rich since he refused to pay attention in school. Then he said. ' *I don't have to go to school to be rich, I would marry a very wealthy old woman, and do something that shocks her, she dies of heart attack and I will inherit her money*"

" he really said that?" completely stunned

" yes. I was surprised myself. How can a little boy of that age reason like that" laughing out loud. Malik sits next to her" surely his elder bothers influence" she said

" yeah," he smiled at the angel beside him. Knowing that she was finally happy, overwhelmed him. The first time Malik met Lara, he instantly noticed a lot of things about her, due to how observant he was. He could tell, she was scared, especially when one approached her, she wasn't comfortable with body contact, didn't do well with crowds and always carried a blank expression, her smiles were mostly fake. For someone who couldn't remember anything but still had such behaviour means that she had gone through so much that even in the absence of those memories of events, her body still reacted in such a way.

That is something that called his attention to her, other than her beauty. She was curious and that curiosity instantly turned into uncontrollable feelings towards her. Malik promised himself that he would make her happy during the little time she had with him and thank goodness, he could see deference and it was just a wonderful sight

" what are you doing?" calling him back to reality

" Nothing" shaking his head

" Don't look at me like that" nervously

" why" he grins

" because I don't know what it means" she spoke seriously, changing the mood

" I don't understand"

" whenever you look at me like that, it is like you are trying to tell me something and I don't know what it is" Malik busts into laughter, at her cuteness and she frowns

" really? Does it bother you" laughing

" It is not funny" she scolded, immediately he stopped, noticing that she wasn't pleased

" am sorry" sounds serious as well

" it is not funny. If you want to say something to me just say it and don't confuse me"

" I'm sorry OK" staring into her eyes trying to calm her down" You will get to know what it means soon, and I will be waiting" says. Now Lara Became more confused.

" why are you here anyway"

"oh" remembering he came for a purpose" so I will be going on a business trip with Rebecca tomorrow"

" tomorrow? Where ?" surprised

" California. And I want you to come with us, with me to be honest"

" oh" more surprised" wasn't expecting that"

" I was thinking if you want your memories back it won't be easy to get them when you are locked up here. Maybe if you go out we will definitely come across things you will be familiar with. something that can bust your memory. And also I wanted us to go out, do something fun"

" I will love that". bit her lower lips, holding back her smile.

****

They left for California as early as 5 am using the family's private jet. Arrived an hour and 30 minutes later. They booked a hotel for the next one week they will be staying not to forget Lara was stunned when she found out that the hotel was owned why the family along with 15 other buildings in California. Which explained so much about their wealth.

Malik and Rebecca left for the meeting immediately, promising her that the moment they returned he would take her out, somewhere nice." Guinevere" Cordelia called from outside while she took a shower.

" yes ?" she responded. trying to wash the soap out of her face, preventing it from getting in her eyes" what is it?"

" I thought we agreed on going out" she sounded desperate

" well why do you think I am taking a shower" reminded her just in case she wasn't aware

" It is taking so long. I am not getting any younger" she scolded and her words reminded her of Lady Thalassa

" why do you sound like mother"

" because she is my mother. My aunt, but still my mother"

" whatever" turning up the hot water" I will be out soon"

" just hurry up"

In a few minutes, she was out and in the bedroom where Cordelia watched her get dressed. In the past, she would feel awkward, but with time she has gotten used to it without even realizing it. She had no idea she had gown so close to Cordelia.

" so where are we going" sat on the bed next to Cordelia

" Sea-world" Cordelia leans forward with excitement in her tone

" sea-world" whispers the word under her breath, In deep thought." sounds familiar"

" well it was among the places I told you about yesterday" shrugs" maybe that is why it sounds familiar

" probably" Cordelia took out her phone and showed Lara pictures of the place" what do you say"

" it looks like a place for kids"

" It is not and we are going"

****

The sun had almost set. On their way back, Laughter and charting filled the car. Talking about the splendid time at sea-world. Cordelia kept emphasizing on the first ride which Lara didn't find friendly." sorry but I just can't help it"

" don't blame me. It was my first ride my body had to adjust. I didn't panic like that on the second ride"

"That was because the second ride wasn't that high" she said in the middle of her laugh. They Laughed so hard that the taxi driver frowned. It got to a point that it became a bit silent and Lara was the only one laughing"

Guinevere ?" there was a sudden change in Cordelia's tone when she called her name.

" yes?" putting her laughter on hold.

" I am going back to school in two weeks" she forced a smile

" oh. Yes, you did tell me you were in your final year." nodding" but is that what is bothering you?" leans in noticing that there was more she wanted to say.

" I don't know if I will ever see you again" she finally let out. The muscles in Lara's face relaxed

" why will you say that? Won't you come back ?"

" I would but what about you? Master already told me" she says sadly" he has been trying to get tips from me on how to get you to stay but it seems like there is no changing your mind"

" oh" A long silence between them. her eyes fell on the driver who didn't seem to care about what they were talking about

" why don't you like Malik?" Cordelia's question took Lara by surprise

" I didn't say that"

" if you do then why do you want to leave? The people are already fond of you, the children always come around for your stories, the mother loves you, and father is already anticipating his grandchildren and I... I like you a lot Guinevere. Malik..." she hesitates" Malik is in love with you and it's like you have no idea"

" in love?" shocked. Malik loved her? And didn't say anything?" Cordelia.."

" why don't you like Malik?" she asked again" You have no idea how he acts whenever I am against him helping you. You know just the other day he almost cried. He said that he doesn't know why you won't give him a chance"

" You are kidding right?" Cordelia gave her a very unpleasant look. This was the first time Cordelia had shown anger towards Lara" you are not being fair Guinevere" disappointment in her words

" Cordelia, I do like Malik" Cordelia's eyes brightened a little" I mean who wouldn't, he is sweet, honest, sometimes too honest" gave a short laugh" I love his sense of leadership, his love for the most little thing, his relationship with the people and how he plays with children and animals. His relationship with the family, especially his sister." she thought about their little fights

" yeah the two love each other" Cordelia whispered with a faint smile

"I like the way he cares, Cares about me. Always want to put a smile on my face and make sure I am pleased. And how he resolved augments with me"

" so what is the matter?"

" I don't know, I don't know what is wrong with me. I actually wanted to leave at the beginning because I can't marry a man I barely know but now I don't know any more"

" fine," The taxi then stopped in front of the hotel and without any more words Cordelia paid the driver, got out and began walking away. That night the two didn't speak to each other.

****

It was past nine. A sudden knock on her door. She pulled herself up from the bed and made her way to the door. With hopes that it was Cordelia. But no. it was him, dressed in a nice black suit with his hair nicely down. Damn, he looked so fine. She tried to hide the joy on her face with a confused look" wow" scanned him from head to toe. Also noticed he had something behind him." Questions. when did you return? Why are you dressed like that? And what are you hiding" spoke quickly

" I returned like 2 hours ago, I wanted us to go out and eat and I got you this" he reveals a well-packaged box. Lara took it from him with confusion written all over her face. She opened the box to see a pretty white dress. He watched as she unfolded the dress and no words could explain how happy she felt by the beauty of the dress. A simple and perfect kneel-level dress

" oh" speechless. Her warm gaze fell on the man in front of her, the man who happened to be in love with her

" do you like it?" he sounded a bit nervous. Using his hand to scratch the back of his neck

" I love it" grins"Malik"

" yes?"

" you are doing too much for me, I don't think I can ever repay you"

" you can, by wearing the dress and having this one night with me" not taking his eyes away from hers

" OK" Nods

" perfect"

In an hour, They were heading for one of the best restaurants in California. Throughout she listened to Malik talk about the meeting and how he got bored of sitting in the same room with those rich folks people, she had to remind him times without number that he was also rich folk

they arrived at the restaurant and Malik opened the door for her like a gentleman that he was. Lara could not take her eyes off the building" stunning right" he whispered in her ear

" No, I mean yes, but" with eyes focused on it. There was something familiar about the place, very familiar. She has been here before, not once but on countless occasion

"But what?" waiting for her to finish her sentence. She turns to look at him only to notice the concerned look in his eyes.

" it...." Lara hesitate. She didn't want to spoil the night for Malik with her problems so she chose to remain silent about it, maybe tell him later" never mind" with a smile

" Guinevere what is it?" he didn't look like he was going with never mind. she slowly took his hand in hers and grins

"let's eat first, we'll talk later" It took him a while to finally agree with a nod and with that, they walked into the restaurant holding hands

****

" it looks nice" said in a low tone from across the table to Malik as they sat silently waiting for a waiter to come attend to them. A fancy place, filled with couples and business people. The lighting was stunning, beautiful chandeliers, the interior decoration, was splendid and the waiters were all nicely dressed.

" it does" he nods in agreement" I have always wanted to come here"

" why haven't you?"

" you know," shrugs" I wanted to come with someone special and here we are" his words made her heart flutter. she looks away from him feeling angry with myself. After all of this, she would leave him." are you alright" Malik asked

" I think Cordelia is upset with me" she said, expecting him to be shocked but he wasn't

" I know" he says

" oh..... how is that?"

" I went to see her to ask about the dress and Cordelia is not the type to hide things from me" Adjusting himself in his seat. Looking reluctant about the whole thing. She stared at him. If he knows, that means he knows what happened and is pretending like it is nothing, this made her frown

" then why are you not saying anything"

" what should I say? Cordelia will get over it by tomorrow"

" not that" she said and hesitated" You love me" his smile dropped" Cordelia told me that you are in love with me and what I don't get is why you are still being nice to me, why you are still helping me when you know that if I get my memories back I will leave you. I will hurt you"

" right" he forced a smile" I guess I'm stupid......" nodding" I can't force you to do what you don't want to do, I can't force anyone to do what he/she doesn't want to do"

" Malik that is bullshit OK."

" well, what do you want me to do? I should force the marriage on you. What difference will it make? Would you like me if I did that" he remained calm

"oh" in a low tone.

" you would hate me if I had forced you to marry me and that, I can not take that. So I thought it would be better to help you out since that is what you want and maybe along the line you will get to like me, remember I said this in the beginning"

" why did you tell Dr Alex that I am your future wife?"
" Because you are"
'" Don't be ridiculous I said the matchmaker made a mistake

"the matcher maker does make mistakes"

" I thought you also don't want to marry me"
" When did I say that"
" You said you said you were helping me to help yourself."
" I am. Helping you means getting to spend time with each other and who knows what will happen from there. And to be honest, I already had a thing for you before the matchmaker said anything"

" you said that you will help me with hopes that I will change my mind"

" I guess I was wrong" he smiled sadly, disappointment written in his eyes" You know I was a bit too confident. thought I would be able to get you to like me because I had a lot of girls falling for me. But for the first time, the girl I actually like doesn't like me back. It is very funny" laughing nervously. At that point she wanted to tell him that it wasn't true, she did like him but what difference would it make?

" Malik I.." just then they were cut off by the waitress

" good evening sir" she greeted Malik who nodded in response" Good evening madam" her eyes fell on Lara and immediately it went wide open" Madam!!" called out loud, excitedly, calling attention and Lara raised an eyebrow at her in confusion

" do you.... know me?" the question rolled out of her lips, at that moment she didn't know if she was glad to see someone who recognised her or not

" of course, I know you. You are........"

Lara?" A shocked voice echoed in her ear giving her this feeling. This familiar feeling of anger mixes with a lot of other emotions. Lara turns around to see who it is, only to be met with that face. A very familiar face, long straight black hair and forest green eyes. The Lady stared at her like she'd seen a ghost. While Lara was filled with confusion, staring at the Lady trying to remember where she had seen that face before and why she felt this way towards her." how are you...." The lady couldn't finish her sentence. She just stood there panting, terrified

" who are...." Lara's questions stopped mid-way as it hit her hard" Davina ?" her forehead squeezed due to confusion, as the name rolled out of her lips" Davina" she whispered the name under her breath once again and boom the world around her began to spin" aaaaaaa" taken by unbearable pain. her head ached terribly, that she didn't even realize she had reached the ground.

" Guinevere!!!" she heard Malik's Panicking tone as he rushed over to her"Guinevere!" he called again but this time it sounded faint. Feeling dizzy, everything blurs" Guinevere". The next time she opened her eyes Malik rushed her into the car" *Guinevere you will be alright I got you*" Then she went blank.

CHAPTER

11

Rebecca

Rebecca sat on her bed with her eyes focused on her laptop while her fingers explored the keyboards. She suddenly gets an email from the one person she has been waiting for and almost immediately her phone rings. Rebecca takes the call putting it on speaker so she could view the email at the same time

"We finally found her. I just sent her details to you" the person spoke from the other end

" thank you. I will get back to you" with that she ends the call. Rebecca opens the email and Lara's picture appears followed by her details." Omolara" she whispered the name to herself" strange name you have"Rebecca reads the details and she gave a short smile" I see you are a Nigerian" nodding her head" time to go back home Omolara" just then she was interrupted by endless knocking on her door" Damn it" she yelled in anger" who is it?"

" It's me" it was Cordelia. Rebecca rolled her eyes wondering what Cordelia wanted with her. She thought she had become best friends with Guinevere. Rebecca made her way to the door, and opened it only to see Cordelia panicking" what!"

" Malik and Guinevere are at the hospital" Hearing Malik was in the hospital made Rebecca show a little interest

" what happened?"

" I don't know I think Guinevere passed out or something"

" oh" an instant relief wash over her" I will get my jacket.

****

Davina

She sat at the back of the car biting her fingernails in deep thought. She was told that the job was done, she was told that she was dead and it has been over two months now. Why is she suddenly alive" stop the car" she says to her driver with anger in her tone

" but miss...." she cut him off

" I said stop the fucking car" yelled at the top of her voice immediately he did as he was told" Now get out" With no questions asked the young man got out of the car. Rolled up all the glass so she would be left alone" fuck! Fuck!! Fuck!!!!!!" screams" Ha,aha" panting. Davina reached for her phone and dialled that number. It rang a few times until the person finally picked" you mother fucker!!!!" she yelled

" good evening to you too" that familiar Italian accent spoke in a mocking tone from the other end.

" you said the work is done, you told me she was dead and you took my money" she yells again.

" would you calm down"

" don't you dare tell me to calm down"

" am sorry but if you are not calm I won't understand what you are saying" the two were taken by silence

" fuck you" she broke the silence sounding calm

" I love you too. Now which one are we talking about?"

" Lara. The Nigerian writer" said

" oh the black beauty"

" don't you call her that" irritatedly" why is she still alive?"

" that is not possible I blew up that plane myself" finally sounding serious

" then why is she alive? Did you find her body?"

" how do you expect me to find her body in an ocean like that? Do I look like a Marine or something?"

" you fucked me and took my money and still didn't get the job done. I told you to make sure she was gone"

" And I did" he began to grow irritated as well" but it looks like the big guy above doesn't want her gone yet"

" is that what you are going to say to me" shocked and disappointed

" look love. I will look into it and see what I can do" with that he ended the call

" fuck!!!!!!!!!!" she screamed in frustration" this is not good" says to herself." but where have she been all this while"

****

Lara

A Memory

The crowd gathered as Mr James stepped forward with Lara by his side. Davina stood somewhere in the crowd as she watched with a small smile. She was amazed by how this young Nigerian lady made it up to the top so fast. This girl was a perfect match for her.

" I stand here today proud to present Omolara. Our new finest writer who has made it to the top 10 world screenwriters in just a year" he announced"

give it out to Omolara" the crowd began to clap in celebration. Some came to pull her in for a hug while others shook her hand and she smiled at all of them in return feeling overwhelmed by the much body contact. She needs to get out of here, out of this crowd before she gets another PTSD attack.

" thank you"

" it will be a pleasure working with you" a Lady said as she took her hand. That was when she first saw her. Davina.

" the pleasure is all mine" she forced a smile

" what do you say about a duo on my next story? It will be lovely to have someone like you assist me just imagine what we can create," she said

" that is a lovely offer but I have no intentions of working with anyone. I work alone"

" that is quite ambitious of you. I like that, we will relate very"

" I hope so" With that Lara walked away not giving Davina a chance to say anything else. Mr James caught her the arm, preventing her from leaving.

" where do you think you are going?"

" home. It's getting late"

" oh come on. You just made me billions and you think I will let you off without a celebration. We are having a party right now"

" I am sorry to disappoint you but I don't celebrate. You guys should go on without me" she pulled her hand off his. At this point, everyone had eyes on her but she didn't care, she just wanted to get away from them, away from people. She has had a long day and needs her pills to calm her nerves

" don't be like that Lara. Everyone made time to come celebrate your victory and you just want to leave like that?" Davina spoke as she stepped out of nowhere

" I....."

"It's just one night. It won't kill you even if it is for an hour or two" Davina said as their gaze met. The room went silent while Lara thought.

" I'm sorry but I can't force myself to do what I don't want to. I will make it up to everyone" she walks away ignoring everyone's murmur.

<u>*Another memory*</u>

" Daddy please" Lara begged in tears for freedom. But no, he won't let her go, not until he gets what he wants. He threw her to the wall and she fell in pain still trying to get up and fight, knowing too well it was pointless." *Daddy am sorry"*

" You dey mad? You think say you fit run from me" he grabbed both arms and began dragging her to the room

" no I didn't" she carried as her body moped the floor while he dragged" *No, please"*

" you dey crazy for head. I will show you that you are mine"

" aaaaaaa" screaming for help. But there was no one, no one was coming to her rescue and it has always been that way. He gets to the room and throws her on top of the bed. She tried to get up immediately, but he got on top of her using one hand to hold her both hands while he unlashed his belt and tied her both hands to the bed." *Daddy please"*

" shut up" punched her face and she weakened instantly. Panting, he looked down at his pretty little girl, while he tried to calm himself" *oh sweetheart"* leans closer, so close that their lips were inches away. The smell of alcohol grew unbearable as he spoke" *You know I love you"* he adjusted her wavy hair which covered her face. She was just like her mother.

" Daddy don't do this"

" I love you my dare and I will never hurt you"

" daddy please ......"

" shuuuu" he placed his finger on her lips shutting her up" e no go pain you if you no struggle"

" I promise I won't try to run away again"

" no... you talk the same thing yesterday and here we are" he leaned in and kissed her neck" I no go waste time" he gave that smile, that smile she has grown to hate more than anything

" Daddy please" she cried in a much lower tone and watched as he ripped her clothes apart, took off his trousers and rushed her like a tiger going for its prey. Once again it happened, he rapped her, she cried for help but no one came, no one wanted to know what was happening. She walks on the street and feels people staring, they knew, they knew what was happening to her but they never came, they never cared. She had once asked a boy for help to run away but he wanted something in return, Her body. She asked a woman but turned out to be the wrong person, instead of helping her. She went on to do what we Nigerians call [amebo] to another woman and somehow her father found out making things worse. If only her mother never left. If only her mother was here to protect her. Or if only her mother took her along with her

****

Back to reality

"Bip, bip, bip, bip" that sound kept repeating itself. Lara opened her eyes. The environment blurred at first but became clear after a few blinks. Hospital. She realized that she was in the hospital." Guinevere" that familiar voice called with worries in his tone. He suddenly appeared above her and Lara smiled at the sight before her.

" Malik" the name rolled out of her lips weakly

" oh thank goodness" Cordelia suddenly appeared on the other side as she took her hand and gave it a slight squeeze" I was so worried" she had a relieved expression" I will get the doctor" immediately ran out of the room.

" Guinevere are you alright" Malik adjusted her hair" Does it hurt anywhere" looking so worried. She didn't respond, she just kept staring at him. Staring at the man who claimed to love her and wondered what he would have done, would he have been different from others in her past? would he have saved her from her father if by coincidence he happened to be around during that time? What if he was just like that other? What if he only says he likes her now because he wants her body like other men?" Guinevere" He calls snapping her out of her thought

" yes?"

" I said does it hurt anywhere"

" yeah. My head" she managed to say" but I will survive" trying to sit up that was when she noticed Rebecca's presence in the room. She sat at the other end of the room with arms crossed watching like she wasn't there" Rebecca" a small smile appeared on her lips but Rebecca rolled her eyes in response taking Lara aback.

" well you are alive, Malik is happy. I guess I will take my leave now" she stood up and reached for her phone on the table beside her" see you later she said to Lara and left

" what happened?" Lara asked with an eyebrow raised

" ignore her. the doctor will be here soon"

****

The doctor arrived and assured them that she was okay and would be discharged tomorrow. Malik left to go get her some food while Cordelia left to who knows where.

Standing by the window with eyes set outside. This familiar city. When she first came to this city she thought that it would finally be over, a new beginning, she would finally be away from her past. Be alone with no one bothering her. Just her and her career but she was wrong. Her past hunted her every night and every day. She sees that face and that smile that she despises so much. Also, people hated her just because she was a black Nigerian. Her co-writers wanted her to fall and her friend accused her of being a criminal when she was the one guilty *Davina.*

A fake smile cut across her lips as her stupidity rang in her head. She couldn't believe that she had tried so hard all this time to remember a life that she had always hated. She finally got a second chance, a chance to be happy away from everything that had happened but she chose to remember. It would have been better if she didn't. She won't be filled with all this pain, hatred, anger and sorrow once again.

" Guinevere ?" Lara was brought out of her thoughts by Cordelia who she had no idea just walked in. She turns around to see the young lady standing in front of her confused" shouldn't you be in bed?"

" I am tired of staying in bed" spoke blankly

" I see" nodded in understanding." Guinevere?" she took a step closer" about last night" Lara was suddenly reminded of that night in the taxi

" forget about it, you said what you had to say"

"no, I shouldn't have. Malik spoke to me last night and he was right. We shouldn't force you to do what you don't want to. I myself won't like that" forced a smile" it's just that everyone likes you already, I don't even want to imagine how sad Mother will be when she finds out...."

" Cordelia can you please leave" Cordelia was dumbfounded. She did expect Lara to suddenly send her out in that manner

" Pardon?"

" oh sorry" realizing the tone she used" I mean I don't want to talk right now, I need time to be alone, to think about this whole thing"

" oh" nodding her in understanding" I should leave you then"

" I will appreciate that"

" but are you feeling ok?"

" yes am fine, why ?" with an eyebrow raised

" nothing, it's just that you suddenly sound different" She took a step back while giving Lara a full scan" this strange aura around you that I can't explain" Lara grew confused

" aura?"

" forget about it" she said" See you later" With that she walked out of the room. Leaving Lara staring at the door for a while, after she left Lara flashed back to the first day she met her

"And you are?....."
" Cordelia" she carried a warm smile. walks up to the table and places the bow of water on it" so how are you feeling?"

"Who knew we would be this close" She smiles. Lara was about to turn around when the door opened again. thinking that it was Cordelia she lifted her head. it wasn't Cordelia but Rebecca" Hey?" confused as to what she was doing here" I thought you already left?"

" I had to wait for the others to leave, I needed to talk to you"

" what about" Lara watched her reach for her jacket pocket and brought out her phone. She tapped on the screen a few times then handed the phone over to her

" what is.." before she could finish her sentence her eyes fell on the picture. It was her, she screwed down to see her details. So Rebecca has been busy she thought to herself. She never would have guessed that Rebecca had time for things like this" you were helping?"

" helping myself actually" with a frown" Omolara is your real name, you are from Nigeria. Hah" she gave a short laugh" started writing at the age of 16 and at 18 you had already become famous for your work. Somehow you attended New York Film Academy and began writing and directing movies. But your writing career was more effective than your directing so you decided to focus on that. Became one of the best in your industry and made it to the top 10. Wow" she nodded impressed Everything was going well, then you got arrested for infringement right and after a while of investigation, you were found innocent. Then people began to complain about the ending of your stories, then it was announced that you were going on a break and that was when they heard from you last. I am guessing that's when the plane crash happened"

" some investigation you did here" Lara was impressed as she handed the phone over to Rebecca who seemed confused at her reaction" also it is pronounced Omolara with a short O, not OmOlara a long O, and I started writing at 15 few months before I turn 16" smirked

"you...you remembered? Have you been pretending?" DUMBFOUNDED

" Don't be ridiculous why will I suddenly want to pretend to lose my memory" she walked up to the bed and sat down, placing both hands behind her as she leaned backwards with legs crossed

" When did you get them back"

" before I ended up here" smirked

" so" Rebecca steps forward

" so ?"

" you are leaving right?.Besides that is what you said on the first day. that you didn't want to marry Malik that is why you have to get your memories back so you can leave" Lara flashed back to that day

" wait you went this far just because of Malik" Lara was in shock" You don't like me because I am to marry Malik ?"

" you don't like Malik and I know"

" I never said that."

" you don't have to, If you did you wouldn't want to leave. But it is for the best. So now it is over, you got your memories back, end things with Malik and leave us"

" and if I don't want to"

" you don't belong on that Island OmOlara"

" I said it is pronounced Omolara and people call me Lara"

" I don't care what they call you. I just want you out of my sight, out of that Island and out of Malik's life. This is where you belong, you have a rich, famous life right here, so don't be greedy" Her voice grew louder

" do you think Malik will be OK with that?"

" that is none of your concern. You got your life back now, leave us alone." with that she walked out shutting the door behind her.

Lara sat on the bed as a million thoughts ran through her head. Rebecca was right, this is what she wanted. She wanted to go back to her past life to avoid marrying Malik and now she remembers everything why was she thinking twice? She should just end things with Malik right now and go back home. *Home?* That word sounded strange. Did she ever have a home? No, she never did.

It was that moment it hit her. She had grown attached to the people of that island without even realizing it. She didn't even realize when she became comfortable with crowds and body contact. It was like her PTSD was totally gone. In The 26 years of her life that Island has become like home to her than anywhere else and now she wants to leave it behind and go back. Besides she never belonged there. She only ended up there by accident. Can she leave these people? Lara lay down with her eyes closed trying to get some sleep maybe she will be able to get her mind off things.

CHAPTER

12

"When are we leaving?" Lara suddenly asked Malik. It has been two days since they returned from the hospital and Lara hasn't stopped thinking. She did some research only to find out that she had been announced missing. The police were still investigating while Davina returned to the industry. Lara wasn't surprised James took her in. He has always been a lover of money. Always on the side that favours him and her missing will do him a great loss which he won't be able to risk. Lara has been thinking of going back, going to face Davina and also finding out what happened on that plane, why the pilot suddenly die

Malik on the other hand had noticed Lara's sudden change of behaviour, she was back to her lifeless mood. Like she was when she first came to the Island

" you seem not to like this place, why?"

" I just wanted to know when we will be going back"

" did you remember something?" he took a step forward with curiosity in the look he gave" You have been acting odd" She looked away immediately not wanting to look him in the eyes" Is it a memory?" he took a few more steps closer

" It is nothing"

" no, it's not. that woman?" he finally asked the question he had been wanting to ask since they left the hospital. He didn't ask earlier because she never brought it up. But seeing that woman, landed her in the hospital.

" Malik..."

" who is she ?" cutting her off. now standing in front of her making it difficult to resist eye contact" Guinevere ?" he calls calmly" What did you remember?" there was a long silence between them. Malik stared at her, waiting for an answer

" Don't make me lie to you Malik" finally spoke

" then don't" his voice remained calm as always

" I don't want to tell you yet until. I figure things out" looking down away from his eyes

" so it is a memory?" her silence was enough to give him an answer" How much ?" she remained quiet for a while

" much"now looks up, again meeting his gaze" Everything" There was this sudden look Malik gave like he was hurt or something but Lara didn't understand.

" so?"

" I don't want us to talk about it. Give me time to think it through, Malik. Please"

" ok" nodding his head" Well we should hang out later when I return what do you think?" she raised an eyebrow at him at his sudden change in topic

" you are going out?"

" I have to finalize the business deal today so I will be out for a while. Do something with Cordelia. She tells me that you two have not really been having much conversation and it keeps her worried" He walks towards the bed to grab his suit jacket. She smiled as she realized that he was changing the topic because she said she needed time to think." I mean it, do something with her" sounding like a parent

" ok"

" good. See you when I get back" he winked and blew a kiss at her before leaving her standing there smiling.

****

Standing in front of Cordelia's room door. She hesitates to knock. they truly haven't talked much since the hospital. After almost 10 minutes of standing there the door suddenly opened taking her by surprise. She could also see the shock in Cordelia's eyes as well

" Guinevere ?" panting as if she had just seen a ghost but Lara remained calm." Goodness you scared me"

" I see you are dressed" She scanned Cordelia from head to toe" Going out?"

" Actually going to your room to see if you want to go out and do something, I am tired of sitting in all day" She smiled at the lady in front of her, who is always in the mood to do something

" yeah I will love that"

" ok. Let's go out" Cordelia took Lara's hand and began leading her to the elevator

" so where are we going?"

" I don't know but we decide on the way"

****

Sanding outside the hotel with no destination. The both of them looked at themselves then back at the busy road" Should we get a taxi" Cordelia asked and Lara gave her this look that said, are you alright?

" and tell the driver what?"

" oh right. I forgot" tap her forehead" do you have anywhere in mind? Oh sorry you don't have any"

" Actually, I do"

" really? where ?" an eyebrow raised

" at Sunset Boulevard"

" you know a place there ?" stunned

" a long story. Tell you later" They got a taxi and Lara gave him the full address. They reached Sunset Boulevard and she led the way.

" where are we going?" Cordelia asked as she noticed the endless trees and dark woods with not a single building in sight.

" We are almost there" she announced

" I can't see any houses"

" that is because there is only one" There was this look Cordelia gave her but she just focused on the road until they finally arrived. The only house on the street. A white mansion.

" why will someone own a mansion in the middle of the woods"

" It is not literarily the middle of the woods"

"Rich folks and their bullshit"

They got out and Cordelia paid the man, then came to join Lara where she was standing in front of the black gate.

" who's place is this anyway ?" Lara didn't respond. She just kept staring at the building debating to herself if she should go in or not." Guinevere?" calling her back to reality

"This is my house" Her words made Cordelia speechless with eyes wide open as she realized that it only meant one thing.

" you.... Do you remember?"

" yes. Yes, I do" Cordelia watched her put in the security code and the gate opened. without hesitation, Cordelia walked in, in a hurry to see the place while She followed slowly behind her. She put in the the code of the front door and led Cordelia in this time

" wow this is beautiful" Cordelia announced, eyes exploring the house. A white house, with furnitures a mixture of black and white. A lot of things were made of glass and from where they stood they could see the backyard through the glass wall. Covered with carpet grass." can I?"seeking permission to explore the place

" yeah, whatever" shrugs in a low tone. With that Cordelia wondered of to who knows where.

Lara stood in the middle of the house looking around. This house, this empty house has always been her escape space from everything. After a long day, she always returns here, takes a shower, feeds herself and spends the rest of her day in the library. She never got a maid or anything, so she could always be busy cleaning, cooking, washing and not get bored. She had a pool on the other side of the house which she cleaned herself and whenever she succeeded at something she would celebrate there all by herself and never hosted a party. The quiet life she prefers, she never realized that she was lonely.

She made her way to the library, Her favourite space. It was dark, very dark. Her hand robbed the wall looking for the light switch which she found and lit the space up. Strolling past several shelves. The library was big enough to be called a Community Library. There were deep black areas of the library which proves how large it was. The main place she gets away from the world, from everything. Whenever she came here she is finally able to forget her sorrow and put that energy into creativity.

" wow," she was interrupted by that familiar voice. She moved away from one of the shelves so she would be able to see the surprised-looking Cordelia." this is a national library"

" Don't be dramatic" with a smirk she began walking forward

"whatever. It is big for a single person, I can see the depth of the room" Cordelia pointed in the direction that had no light

" that is where I put books that I have already read"

" ok. Wow" she looked at Lara who was now leaning quietly against the table" so, what is going on?" Cordelia had a serious tone as she sought an explanation

"My name is Omoralra Lovett Tosin. I am half Nigerian half Australian. 26-year-old Movie writer and director. Well, I didn't really enjoy directing because it has to do with too many people so I quit. And this is my home, more like just a house now"

" you..... Do you remember everything?" Lara nodded in response to Cordelia's question." when?"

" before I ended up in the hospital and also in the hospital"

"This is great" Cordelia announced sounding excited but when she noticed the expression on Lara's face the excitement drained" Isn't it?"

" I don't know" in deep thought" I don't know if it is something to be excited about or not"

" but isn't it what you wanted?"

" hah" she gave a short depressing laugh" that is exactly what Rebecca said"

" Rebecca knows?" an eyebrow raised" you told her before you told me ?"

" she found out on her own"

" that is not right. How?" Lara shrugs at the question

" I don't know and I don't care" Cordelia deep her hands in her jeans pocket with eyes on the ground as she thought for a while" So you are leaving after this?" that question. This is the decision she has been trying to make since she got her memories back

" I don't know. If I am being honest, I do like Malik, a lot. Who wouldn't"

" then don't leave him. I mean you can keep being who you are and still marry Malik. Right?"

" but do I belong there, that island and also a lot are holding me back"

" what is all this bullshit, you do not belong. how? The people have already welcomed you there as your home and now you are wondering if you belong there?" Cordelia was lost" Do you have any idea how much they like you"

" I am scared"

" of what?" throwing hands in the air almost frustrated" I don't get it" There was a long moment of silence between them. Lara stared into Cordelia's eyes wondering if she should speak." what are you scared of" a few minutes went by before she began

" I was very little when her father's business went under. My mother could not take it so she ran off when I was 9, my father fell into depression and started drinking and because of the love he had for my mother, he went crazy and always said I looked a lot like her. Then he will say things to me that I shouldn't hear and touch me in places where he shouldn't touch. As I grew older I began to look a lot like her and this only got things worse for me. Whenever he comes home drunk I try to run away from him, I try to hide but he always found me, he always did no matter how hard I tried. I always fought back but it was useless. even when I cry for help no one ever comes, no one ever comes to save me. he will rape me until I am almost lifeless then leave." she gave a sad smile at the thought of the memory" At 15 years I sold some of the properties at home and ran away thinking that it will be over but it wasn't. Things only got worse. I was always hungry, alone, scared of falling asleep due to nightmares, running away from men that wanted to have sex or rape me. It turns out being a homeless mix bread in a country like Nigeria makes you a prey, to every man in sight."

" that is sad" Cordelia spoke with a very low tone as she looked at Lara with hurtful eyes" No one took you in ?"

"Someone did" She looked at the ground as the memory continued to flow" Madam Rachel. She had a daughter and two sons. In exchange for food and where to sleep I will work in her restaurant for free. She said with looks like mine I would be able to attract customers which I did. Her daughter and I became very close. Back then she was in junior secondary school and that was when I was introduced to novels. Madam Rachel always got her daughter a new novel whenever she returned from work and I made sure I read every single one of them. For a girl who didn't finish primary school, it was a bit difficult at first but I became better with words and developed a love for stories. I was amazed by the way an author creates worlds, characters, plots, and actions, turning it into a story. And also I realized that reading these stories got me away from everything. At that moment I am lost even if it is for an hour or two. It felt nice" Cordelia bit her lower lips" I thought that maybe I would finally be alright here" faked a smile" but I was wrong. One night I was attacked by both sons, I fought and screamed for freedom but luck was never on my side. They ravished me the way my father does" At that moment she couldn't hold back and let her tears flow. Cordelia was about to step forward but she lifted her hand instantly stopping her at track" Don't" in a low tone

" what did their mother do about it" with curiosity in her tone. And sympathy in her eyes

" I was taken to the hospital for sure and left there but before leaving she threatened me not to show my face in front of them again. accused me of seducing her sons and said that I wanted to spoil her family name" using her thumb to wipe her tears" I guess being beautiful is a crime"

" Guinevere..." Lara cut her off

" don't try to console me"

" ok" nodding" what happened next"

" I went to the house of worship. Maybe I will finally find people who will take me in with pure heart. I went to the Catholic church and the sisters took me in immediately. That was when I wrote my first book."*drowning'*". At first, it was distributed to members of the church for free and people began to request more copies. I was advised by the sisters to start writing as a career. They took me to a school for writing by the time I released my third book I was already making little cash. Finally, things were becoming brighter. The sisters wanted me to join them but I couldn't, I feared that I wasn't pure even when they told me that I was in the eyes of the lord and all that I had gone through did not define me, I still refused." Cordelia watched her walk around the table with her finger to line the edge of the dusty table, proving that it hadn't been used for a while. Lara reached the chair and sat down. The chair also needs cleaning." I wrote more books and every single one was a hit. Then I got a call that they would like to shoot one of my stories as a movie." she smiled" life-changing opportunity. I wrote my first movie, then the second and the third then I went to the New York Film Academy and boom the next thing I knew I was a writing star"

" it turned out well in the end"

" you think, in stories when one becomes successful, they say it is a happy ending but it wasn't. When I came to California I planned to leave everything behind and start over but no. It haunted me every day and night. I see their faces, I see my father in my sleep, I see his face in the face of other men not to forget the feeling of loneliness, sadness, hatred that keeps crawling in my heart. And countless Traumas. The doctor said I had (PTSD). it didn't end there. my fellow colleagues were against me because I was a Nigerian with no standard education. my claimed friend accused me of stealing her work when she was the one who stole mine. After it was exposed the fans harassed me for weeks for something I didn't do. My male colleagues always trying to have sex with me and so many more which leads me to that plane crash. And I know very well that someone was behind it"

" what makes you say that"

" the pilot was killed. A pilot doesn't just die" she says with a very serious tone" now you see why I said I don't belong on that island. My life is filled with so many ups and downs. I am filled with hatred, sadness and anger. I trust no one. No good that comes to me ever last. And I fear" she hesitates" now that I remember everything I fear that it will be the same."

" I don't understand"

" I never trusted men until I met Malik. I never enjoyed associating with people until I met you people. And I am scared to get broken because it will be something that I will never recover from"

" it will never happen. Malik loves you"

" Love fades. Love is something that changes faster than anything and what if Malik suddenly stops seeing me the way he does now? What if he starts to see my flaws"

"Everyone has flaws Guinevere and he knows"

" the people of that island are just amazing, loving and caring and I don't fit"

" you did" she marks

"That was before, when I didn't know who I was and now I do and....."

" who are you?" her voice became calm as she asked

" pardon ?" the question got her deep

" who are you now?"

" I am Omolara"

" is that just who you are?"

" I don't understand"

" what mother taught me is that we define who we are or who we want to be" she says as she takes a few steps closer to the table" if you want to be the writer who still holds on to her past believing she is messed up and push everyone away even the right ones then fine, you can. But you can also be the one who doesn't let her past define who she is and live a happy and peaceful life" she leans down with both hands on the table, eyes locked on Lara's

" I have tried to be that person"

" you haven't. Do you want to know why the people of that island are so carefree? Because we do the most difficult thing. We forgive and let things go, that is when you will be at peace and happy."

" you are telling me to forgive then?" Lara couldn't believe her words

" you have been through a lot Guinevere. And it would have been best if you didn't remember but you did" nodding her head" If you want to be that person then you have to forgive and let go, control your own life. Then those feelings will disappear." there was a long silence in the house. Lara was lost in deep thought while Cordelia watched.

Lara knew Cordelia was right. She may have left the place but the hatred was still there, the anger. Maybe if she finally forgives and lets go it will finally be over. But can she forgive them? Can she forgive him? For making her life a nightmare, can she forgive her mother for leaving her with a monster of a father? can she forgive the people for not helping a girl in desperate need of help? She wasn't sure she would be able to do it.

" We should leave" She broke the silence

" okay but quick question, you live here alone?"

" Yeah" she shrugs as she stood up" Malik will soon be back" walking past her while Cordelia followed behind her

" does Malik know"

" he knows that I got it back but I haven't told him this story,"

" you have to tell him"

" I know. But not now"

****

There he was sitting next to her on the couch. They both watched a movie on his laptop. Malik was already fast asleep on her shoulder while she was completely zoomed out, lost in her thoughts, thinking of what Cordelia and Rebecca said. She didn't have much time left. They will be returning to the Island tomorrow so she has to decide right now if she will be going back with Malik or staying back in California.

If she goes back with him that means that she has agreed to marry him, but what is wrong with that? Her eyes fell on the sleeping young man. The man that she not long found out she has feelings for. She has grown to love him in every way. The man who showed her what it is like to have a family showed her what it is to be happy. She suddenly flashed back to the first night during the chosen festival.

Flashback 1

" I said I don't want to dance"

" is it that you don't like fun or you just don't like happiness"

"happiness" she repeated under her breath.

Flashback 2

" you should smile more often"

" Pardon ?"

" smile more often, most of the time you carry a straight face. No emotion"

" When you say most times it sounds like you have known me long."

" no, I haven't but I remember the first time we met when you entered the kitchen. You had a straight face that honestly frightened me a little and then you said, ' hi ', and to be honest you looked really cute"

"Really?"

" yes. And most of the time your smile is fake. Many may not notice but I do"

" I see"

" And also you look very pretty when do"

" well I will keep that in mind"

Return from flashback

Still staring at him. a thought suddenly came to her mind. What if he only wanted her body? But if he did, he wouldn't be trying so hard to win her heart for marriage, he would be trying to take her to bed instantly" do you really love me" she whispered so low that even a vampier may not pick the sound. That day came to mind again

" what are you doing?"

" Nothing"

" don't look at me like that"

" why ?"

" because I don't know what it means"

" I don't understand"

" whenever you look at me like that, it is like you are trying to tell me something and I don't know what it is"

" really? Does it bother you"

" It is not funny"

" I'm sorry" sounding serious as well

" it is not funny. If you want to say something to me just say it and don't confuse me"

" am sorry OK.... you will get to know what it means soon, and I will be waiting"

" you were trying to tell me you love me?" smiles sadly as she moved his hair from his face gently." I can't believe I couldn't read that. And you waited"

Miya Kwen

CHAPTER

13

A few days after returning to the Island. They were at the ocean side waving Cordelia off for school. Malik and Lara continue to grow closer and this time, She isn't holding back. She haven't told him about her decision to stay, nor have they talked about her memory, Malik was giving her time as he promised. Rebecca on the other hand didn't understand why Lara wasn't leaving. She thought the moment she regains her memory she will leave Malik alone, but it seems like it isn't the case. Instead, the two grew more attached.

" I am going to miss her" Lara whispered to his ear while they watched the ship set sail

" why didn't you tell her" Malik had his eyebrow raised at the lady beside him." you were acting all tough a few minutes ago"

" I just can't bring myself to say it" with a sad look on her face. Malik chuckled. He took her hand and pulled her to his chest gently for a small hug" I wanted to say it but I just couldn't"

" that is the problem with pride" She lifted her head to look up at him with a frown

" what is that supposed to mean?"

" nothing" he bit the edge of his lips and looked away

" did you just say I have pride" still frowning

" I didn't say that" he said pulling her away gently so he could escape

" yes, you did. You said that is the problem with pride. I have pride. Do you …." they were suddenly interrupted by Rebecca who they had forgotten was standing behind them

" Can you two stop acting like children and let's leave" staring hard at Lara" Malik remember we have work to do at the lab"

" I thought you said it was your day off" with disappointment in her eyes

" I did, but something came up a few hours ago" he said while reaching for her hand" but I will be back early for story night. Ok" she only smiles in response

Story night was a tradition for the people of the island. Every last Saturday after three months children will gather at the Fishers mansion to listen to stories and tonight will be Lara's first story night

" ok," she nods.

" thank you for understanding" he smiles" and now my lady" Malik lifts her hand to his lips and with eyes locked to hers his lips brushed the back of her palm smoothly. there was this sudden feeling of electricity that ran through her and she couldn't stop herself from smiling at the young man" I will take my leave"

" ok" nodding. he began walking away with Rebecca behind him. Rebecca turns around and gives Lara this look that says I will end you" what is her problem?" Lara whispers to herself in confusion. Ignoring them She turns around looking to find something interesting to do when she sees Imran with two of his brothers playing in the water. A smile made its way to her lips. The children were having so much fun and she wonders to herself if only she had a fun childhood like this. Her childhood was filled with so many sad memories" Imran!!!!" suddenly pulled out of her thought by Imran's mother who came out of nowhere, walking quickly with anger written on her face"

I thought I told you not to play in the water today" making her way towards them immediately Imran started running and running to Lara's direction" come back here"

" mummy please"

" I said come back here" Imran ran behind Lara, grabbing her shirt for protection

" My Lady, save me" he cried out

" Imran" his mother called with frustration. Trying to reach for her son

" oh my god" Lara lets out. While they pulled her from side to side" madam please..... let him" she struggled to say

" no, I won't, this child needs discipline" still trying to grab him

"Mummy please, I am sorry"

" sorry for your self"

" madam please" trying to calm the woman down" madam"

" no I ..."

" mummy please"

Lara grew frustrated with the two and yelled with so much authority" madam listen" both her hands, on her the woman's shoulders, holding her still. The woman was startled not expecting Lara to raise her voice" please" sounding much calmer" calm down and talk to me" Imran's mother took several deep breaths before she explained

" he is not feeling well" pointing to the boy behind Lara" I told him not to get into the water today it will get worse. But this... this" sounding angry once again

" Imran. Why didn't you listen to your mother?" with an eyebrow raised

" I did but, I mean I was, but Daniel told me that it was ok for me to come out now since I already took drugs"

" Daniel?" eyes wide open

" yes" nodding quickly

" your elder brother ?" she turns in the direction of the boys who were watching the show from where they were playing a few minutes ago." Daniel!!!!" she yells" you are responsible for this?"

"Mummy I didn't know he was still sick"

" come here you idiot" Immediately the two boys started running and she followed. Lara could not hold back her laughter. Was this the feeling of having a mother? If only she did have a mother.

" Imran" she turns to the boy" we better take you home before your sickness gets worse" he nods and takes her hands as they begin heading back to town.

" will you tell us a story today?" he suddenly asked

" I don't know. Maybe"

" I will love it if you do"

****

Rebecca

In the elevator with Malik, silence lived between the two. Malik was scrolling through his iPad while Rebecca watched in silence, wondering what he was doing. Usually, they always had a discussion going but now things have changed, he no longer gives her attention. They no longer talk like they used to. Like they were never childhood friends" what are you looking at?" she goes to stand next to him. She gazed at what he was doing" You want to buy a new phone?"

" yes" he looks at her with a smile then back at the screen

122

" what happened to yours"

" not for me. It is for Guinevere" hearing her name causes pain in her chest. Even in front of her, he only thinks about that woman" she doesn't have one and now that she has her memories back I am sure she will want to speak to a lot of her friends"

" wait" in shock" you knew?"

" know what?" not taking his eyes off the screen

" that she got her memories back"

" yes"

" And you are ok with that?" she frowns, almost yelling

" why shouldn't I be" now he lifts his head, putting down his iPad.

" for goodness sake Malik she is not from here"

" a lot of people on this Island were not from here. why does it upset you?"

" because she is playing you Malik" she yells out of frustration

" I don't understand?" still sounding calm

" she is making you fall for her when in the end she is going to leave this island. Leave you broken" she says." you may think I don't know but I do. She wanted to get her memories back because she didn't want to marry you and for God's sake Malik you were helping. Why?"

" have you been listening to our conversation" now, he was getting angry

"Don't change the topic Malik" she says" You and I both know that what you are doing is a waste of time. She will leave you"

" stop it"

" you know it is true"

" I said stop it" trying to hold himself from raising his voice

" now she got her memories back it is just a matter of time before she announces it to the family and just imagine what Aunt Thalassa would do"

" SHUT. THE FUCK. UP!!!!" finally letting it out. He raised his voice at his best friend, taking her by surprise. This was the first time in the history of their friendship, that Malik had raised his voice at her. There was this strange aura around him as his eyes grew darker, staring at her. Rebecca took a step back out of fear that he might strangle her right that instant.

" you just yelled at me Malik" holding back her tears" because of a woman. A woman who doesn't even know you as much as I do. That has no idea what we have gone through together. You yell at me because of her?" the tears finally flowed

" what I do with her is none of your business. If she leaves in the end, it is none of your business." he says calmly but still angry" But I know that I will keep trying. Trying to get her to love me and even if at the end she leaves, I know that I tried my best" The elevator door opens and he walks out leaving her behind

" Malik" she follows behind him but he ignores" Malik she calls again and this time he stooped. She made her way and stood in front of him

" what if she leave" she asked" would you finally look my way" a long silence lived between them

" I would have?"

" what?"

" I know you were the one who told her to drown herself no matter how you put it" he says

" For God's sake Malik, she is not a child. How would I have known she would take what I said seriously?"

" I know you got someone to do research on her" This took Rebecca by surprise

" what do you..."

" and I also know that you advised her to leave, saying she didn't belong here"

" Malik..."

" don't try to deny it, Rebecca. That will only get me angry" she went silent for a while"

" I can't believe she told on me" Her jaw hardened

" no, she didn't. Cordelia did" startled

" I used to respect you Rebecca." with a death stare" I never expected you to stoop so low" With that he walks away leaving the broken young lady.

" hah" she gave a short, quiet, sad laugh" You have no idea how much I love you Malik" Under her breath she watched him walk away, out of sight.

****

Lara

The story night began. Children of the island gathered in the backyard of the Fisher's mansion. With all the lights in the mansion turned off. The fire was lit they all seated and waited for story time to begin." how long does it last" Lara leaned close to Lady Thalassa to ask

" two hours"

" oh"

" you must be tired due to all the preparation for the night"

" no am fine. Just wondering when Malik will get here" A pleasing smile appeared on Thalassa's lips hearing those words from her

" I see you and my son are beginning to grow attached"

" It is not like that"

" then how is it like"

" how is what like ?" suddenly interrupted by that familiar voice she had been waiting to hear. Malik appeared behind them.

" hey" she smiles brightly

" hey" pulling her in for her hug" sorry I took so long"

" I was becoming tired of waiting" she faked a frown as she pulled away

" I'm sorry. Promise it won't happen again" he raised his hand in surrender

" don't make promises you can't keep"

" grrrrrr" Lady Thalassa cleared her throat calling their attention" I see I no longer exist"

" oh no mother" he pulls her in for a tight hug" am sorry"

" how was your day" she says in his chest

" ok" there was this tone in his voice that said it wasn't ok

" Are you sure?" breaking the hug

" positive"

" if you say so. Let me leave you two" with that she left to join the children" ok everyone. The night has begun" she announced" And I hope you are ready" The two watched with a smile as the story began. Lady Thalassa began and silence lived while she told the story.

" are you alright?" Lara suddenly whispered with a worried tone. He looks down at her with a smile

" yeah. Why?"

" you don't look ok. What happened at the lab" whispers again

" That should be least of your worries" looking back at the children

" but I want to know" calling his attention once again

" come with me" he began walking, She shrugged and followed behind him. Malik leads them to her bedroom and closes the door behind them.

" what is the matter?" with worries in her tone as they stood facing each other. She noticed how nervous he was to say something and this made her smile. Sliding his hand in his pocket with eyes on the ground"Malik, what is it?" with an eyebrow raised

" I..." he hesitates

" I don't read minds, Malik"

" I..." hesitate again" Look Guinevere I wanted to wait until you were ready to talk to me but the longer it takes the more uncomfortable I become so...."

" My real name is Omolara Lovett Tosin. I am a Nigerian Australian" she began, taking him by surprise, he never thought that she would let it out so easily" My father is the Nigeria and my mother, is Australian. I graduated from the New York Film Academy as a movie writer and director. Have you seen the movie" *finding my way?"*

" Yeah" he smiled with amazement

" I wrote and directed that film and many more"

" so you are famous?" he says

" I am"

" ok," in deep thought, nodding while the tried to process the information just thrown at him" Then why didn't you want to tell me? Why did you ask for time"

" there is a lot about me that I hated and I thought you would also not like me for it"

" like what ?"

" My family, my experience with men especially her father" The sudden sadness in her tone told Malik everything

" oh"

" many other reasons that I plan to tell you along the line. Most importantly I wanted to decide" Malik gave her a confused look

" decide ?" an eyebrow raised

" something very important" she smiles

" okay" nodding" and have you decided ?"

" I want to stay" the room went silent and Malik tried to understand what she was saying. It finally clicked and his eyes fell wide open

" you mean?"

" I want to stay with you, Malik. I want to stay with the people of this island. Where I am happy. I want to stay here and......." not able to hold himself back from the overwhelming joy his lips crushed into hers. A surprise kiss, eyes wide open, never in her wide dreams did she expect. Almost immediately she responded wrapping her arms around his shoulder, he pulled her to his body with his hands around her waist. Her lips were soft, wet, sweeter than he had imagined. Her hands explored his hair as the atmosphere suddenly grew hotter. They kissed like it would be their last. Her mind was exploding at this moment, butterflies celebrated in her stomach as she felt his hand exploring her back. Everywhere he touched felt like electricity. So this is what it was like to kiss someone you love, she wondered. She never had good experiences with kisses because of her father. If it wasn't for, Malik who gave her a surprised kiss she would have hesitated, it felt different and just right." ha" A small gasp escaped both of their lips as they broke for air. With faces just an inch apart, she looks down trying to avoid eye contact. Thank goodness she was black, her face would be as red as a tomato right now.

" am sorry" his voice was so low and there was something different about it. It was filled with something she couldn't explain" I found it hard to hold back" bit his lower lips

" hah," she gave a short low laugh" You know from where I come from if we are caught it won't end well" smiling" but you did well. I liked it" She bit her low lips as her eyes fell on his lips. She wanted more. She wanted more of his kiss. She found herself leaning in for another, and so did he. He took her lips again, this time more passionate and deeper. But it didn't last

" Guin dare the children wants....... haaaaaaaa" they were interrupted by Lady Thalassa. They pulled away instantly" oh lord" she shut the door

" oh no" Lara covered her face with her hands out of embarrassment while Malik smiled at her." she caught us" Malik was about to reach for her hands when the door busted open and Lady Thalassa was standing there

" Everyone is outside and you two are here kissing eee?" she scolded

" mother..." Malik was cut off

" don't you mother me. You can't go around kissing even if you are soon to be married" she walks up to Malik" get married already. Do you want to get her pregnant before the marriage? Then what is there to enjoy if you two have sex now"

"Mother" raising his voice at her words while Lara took a few steps back in shock" Don't say things like that" with authority in his tone

" did you just raise your voice at me" startled

" oh no...." before he could react she already grabbed his ear

" aya, aya" being dramatic. Lady Thalassa turns to Lara

" the children want you to tell them a story. I need to disciple this boy of mine" pulling him along with her

" save me" he mouthed to her while she smiled in response. Used her hand to cover her face in embarrassment

CHAPTER

14

Davina

Davina hears a knock on the door of her hotel room. Makes her way to the door wearing only a robe and opens it" you?" shocked to see that familiar face. Dark brown hair, brown eyes, a perfect jawline, with a big scar by the side of his nose. He was 6fit 3, well built. One could see the tattoo on his neck all the way down and vanished into his shirt with his left sleeve also covered in tattoo. He looks down at Davina with a devilish smile

" hello love" that Italian accent sang to her

" what are you doing here?" in a low tone" I thought I told you never to met physically"

" I've missed you love." his eyes travelled down to her exposed legs and his smile widened" I see you are all set" about to lean down to kiss her but Davina walked away leaving him hanging and he followed closing the door behind him

" what happened?" she asked as she sat on the couch with legs crossed

" happened where?" pretending not to know what she was talking about

" don't be an idiot" she frowns

" still got that attitude of yours I see" he sits on the couch opposite hers reaching for the glass of wine on the glass table" Lara" he calls the name before taking a gap from the wine" Nice wine" with an amazed tone" the rich do know how to take nice wine"

" what about Lara?" sounding very impatient. She watched him finish the wine and return the glass to the table

" it turns out there is an Island called Marian Island"

" Marian Island?" she repeated

" You know the place?"

" heard of it. Told it was a lovely place to go on vacation" she says in deep thought

" I agree. We should go there some time"

" Edoardo" she scolds

" ok back to business" raising his hands in surrender" the people happened to rescue her, fortunate on her part and unfortunate for you" he mocked" I did a little investigation and it turns out she lost her memories and was stuck there. And I think she is getting married"

" Married?" with a confusion in her tone

" yes. To the future chief of the Island"

" so?"

" so that is what happened" he shrugs

" I mean what did you do about her"

" nothing." sounding reluctant" what am I suppose to do?" Davina uncrossed her legs and pushed forward

" you are asking me what you are supposed to do" angrily and shocked" am I supposed to tell you to finish the job"

"My job is finished" he smiles" You told me to crash the plane and I did. Fortunately for her, she survived, how is that my business"

" so you are telling me you won't finish the job" she stood up. He lifts his head to look at her with a smile

" I would but I won't do something like that for free"

" you are saying you want another pay?" nodding in disbelieve" are you kidding me now"

" I don't do things for free. But this time I don't need money, I want something else"

" And what is that" crossing her arms

" you" he said as he slowly stood up" After our last I couldn't stop thinking about you" he took a few steps around the table to stand in front of her." I am not asking much. Just one night and the woman will be out of your life for good" he winked then leaked his lower lips as he moved closer covering the space between them

" hah" gave a short disappointed smile and looked away" I guess it is right what they say"

" about what?" with a little bit of curiosity in his tone

" when you want something done, you do it yourself self" now looking into his eyes with pure anger written in hers

" oh. So you want to do it yourself haa" he says stepping back

" yes and I am certain I can do a better job than you"

" oh really" now he got upset" let's see how you get into that Island and kill her, get rid of the body without getting caught"

" I will" she says" now get out"

" oh come on"

" I said get out" raising her voice" don't make me call the securitise"

" you know what, I see why the lord is against you" Moving back" Trust me when I say, you won't succeed" With that he left. Davina made her way to the bedroom and crashed into bed with frustration.

"Just one woman" she whispered with a frown" I am going through all this just because of one woman" Suddenly she gets a beep on her phone. She reached for it on the other side of the bed only to see it was an email. Davina reads through the email and seats up the a smile." interesting" she says

****

Lara

At the kitchen with Lady Thalassa and the cook, preparing dinner when Malik walked in with eyes only on her. A smile made its way to her lips due to the look he gave her and thank goodness she was black if not her face would be as red as a tomato right now." hey" he waved at her

" hey"

" good evening Mother" her greeted his mother as he walked toward her and hugged her" And Love" he looked at Lara who was taken aback at the sudden nick-name. He was about to hug her but she stopped him

" I got flour in my hands" she says in her low tone

" doesn't matter" ignoring her excuse he pulled her for a tight hug, rocking her from side to side while Lady Thalassa smiled at them then went back to what she was doing, and so did the cook

" so.. how did your day go?" Lady Thalassa asked not looking their way

" great. And yours?"

" it went well. Guin is a great company"

" really" he pulls away to look down at her" I see you got you hair done" noticing her new hair style" I like it"

" thank you" smiles" and Rebecca?"

" she is good. But she didn't come home with me. She took 4 days leave from work to go see her cousin in school so she had to go home and pack"

" oh"

" that is disappointing" Lady Thalassa said now looking at them." Everyone is leaving, the house is growing dry" Lara nodded in agreement. The house wasn't as busy as it used to be. Anahita already left for school so did Cordelia and her family. They will only return during the holidays and now Rebecca

" they will come back Mother" with his hands around Lara's waist

" you two should hurry up and get married and give me grandchildren. The house is getting quiet" Lady Thalassa scolded

" mother!!" Malik raised his voice

" did you just raise your voice at me"

" nope" Immediately he let go of Lara and ran out of the kitchen but Lady Thalassa didn't go after him, just laughed at her silly son

" stupid boy" she hissed

" he is not stupid" Lara defended and the look Lady Thalassa gave her made her bit her lower lips in embarrassment

" I get it, you two are in love, definitely, he isn't stupid" rolling her eyes" now get back to work"

" ok"

****

Lara sat on her bed ready to go to sleep when she got a knock on the door." who is it?"

135

" Malik" that familiar voice responded" may I come in?"

" oh yes," she stood up while Malik opened the door and entered holding a big bag" What is that?"

" I....emm" he walks towards her" here" handing the bag over to her. She took it and opened it. There was a big rectangular box inside and a smaller one. He watched her pull out the box and a gasp escaped her lips when she realized what it was

" you got me a Lap top?" with excitement

" yeah, I felt that you may want to continue writing now that you've got your memories back and also interact with the world like normal people" he says

" and a phone" smiling while pulling the other box out

" yeah. You really need that" nodding his head" I just wonder how you have been surviving without it"

" that is so thoughtful of you" she put them down on the bed and gave him a warm hug" thank you"

"Anything for you love" he whispers to her ear and she shyly bit her lips. They remained like that for a while until She finally got the need to break the hug

" you better get back to your room before Mother catches you"

" I don't care" looking down at her" So Love, you are going to keep writing right?" with curiosity in his tone

" I don't know yet, I haven't decided and also I need to go to the bank"

" for what?"

" I have my own money remember. And I can't just leave it for the bank." Malik nodded in agreement" I also need to get my documents, like my ID card, passport, credit card and so on"

" I will see to that"

" thank you" about to kiss him on the cheek but stopped" why the sudden nick name ?" she asked

" oh, that. It is just short for your middle name." Lovett, Love"

" oh" nodding

" I wanted to be the only one that calls you that"

" I see"

" you don't like it?"

" if I didn't I would have told you to stop"

" true" nodding

" you should leave"

" are you sending me away" about to lean in for a kiss but she stopped him by grabbing his shirt and pulling him along with her. She opened the door and sent him outside then shot the door with a smile on her face knowing very what he would do next and he did. She heard a soft knock on the door and her smile grew brighter" Love ?" with a low tone. Lara opens the door to see him standing there looking like a child hungry for candy

"Are you a baby?"

" just one kiss" he said before he could finish, She leaned forward and gave him a quick kiss" Hey that is not fair. I didn't get the chance to do anything"

" you ask for one and I gave you one. Good night and also get your hair done. It is getting messy" changing the subject

" I was thinking, I should cut it short" he said running his hand through his hair

" don't you dare. I love it long. Good night" she shot the door with that same smile again and made her way to the bed

" Good night," she hears him say from outside

138

CHAPTER

15

Rebecca

"Thank you" Rebecca thanked the Taxi driver as he stopped in front of the hotel. Pays him and gets out. Standing in front of the hotel she stares at her phone screen, re-reading the address sent to her. It matched the place" third floor, room 29" she reads. Rebecca makes her way in and straight for the elevator. In about 10 minutes she was standing in front of the room door.

Standing there Rebecca began to reconsider the whole thing. Does she really have to be here? what if she just let it go? What if she just let Lara be? Even if she gets rid of Lara, will she still have a chance, what difference will it make? Malik has never seen her as anything more than a sister and a friend. This is not Lara's fault. She turned around about to leave but stopped at her track. Maybe, just maybe if Lara is out of the picture then Malik will realize that she was right about her and maybe, just maybe there is a chance that he will finally notice her presence and how important she is to him. She has to get rid of Lara.

She turned back around and, without hesitation, rang the doorbell twice. In a minute or two she heard the door opening. Taking a deep breath. In front of her stood that familiar face. The one she saw in the picture. She was even

139

more beautiful in person, with her long dark hair and perfect figure. Rebecca gave a dry smile" good morning"

" Rebecca, right?"

" yes" nodding

" I was expecting you yesterday but nevertheless, come in" Davina says making way for Rebecca to enter and closing the door afterwards." I would love to have a proper introduction but no. business first. No time to waste" she said as they both made their way to the couch.

" I agree" She sits down, placing her handbag by her side

" so tell me" Davina sits opposite Rebecca. Reached for the bottle of wine on the table and began to pure into the two glasses" what is your relationship with Lara" with a faint smile

" she took something that belongs to me" Rebecca spoke with a bit of anger in her tone and this made Davina smile brighter.

" I see" placing the bottle down as she crossed both legs and leaned back" and what did she take?"

" that is my concern."

" if you say so" raising her hand in surrender. She looks at Rebecca and their eyes meet" so why did you call me"

" Because I want you to help me get rid of her"

" and you think I will help you why?" with an eyebrow raised

" I did my research. And of all the things about you that came out one was the top on the list. The case that happened 5 years ago" the smile on Davina's face instantly faded" you and I have a common enemy" she leans forward" I want her out of that island and you want your revenge. We should help each other" there was a long silence between the two as they stared deep at each other. Davina dived into a deep thought for a while. This was a great chance to finally get rid of Lara and she can't just let it slide

" you find a way to hand her over to me. And I will deal with the rest," she said

" she will never return to the island again?"

" it will be like she never existed" She smiled and reached for the glass of wine." cheers" lifts the glass slightly and watched Rebecca reach for the other and they both made a toast

" cheers" followed by the clicking of the glass

****

Lara

" Guin" her name echoed softly in the air by a partially familiar voice

" Guin wake up" echoed again. Lara tried so hard to wake up but it seemed like her sleep didn't want to let go" Guin" the voice grew louder and she knew that this person was not going to let go that easily.

"Mother give me a few minutes" she whined moving the hand off her body

"It is not Aunt Thalassa. It's me, Rebecca ." Rebecca? What? That is not right, Rebecca can't be here. She opened her eyes quickly only to find Rebecca sitting on the bed next to her. She looks around, in her bedroom at Malik's place. How did she get here? She couldn't remember. She only remembered that she and Malik went out to watch the sunset together and she slept off in the car.

" Rebecca?" shocked."what are you doing here. I thought you travelled three days ago?"

" I came back last night"

" okay" feeling awkward" so why are you in my room?"

" I was wondering if you would like to take a walk with me. By the beach"

" you? and me?" Dumbfounded

" yes"

" take a walk? you and me?" very shocked and confused" did you hit your head somewhere?"

" no I didn't" she smiled" why do you sound surprise" mocking Lara's reaction

"Because I am" sitting up" Are you sure you are okay?"

" yes, I am. Will you come with me or not" with a frown

" ammmmm.." looking at Rebecca and feeling uncomfortable about the whole thing. First, it was clear that Rebecca didn't like her, secondly, she never came to her room for favours and also since when did Rebecca want to hang out with her" ok...ay" giving a slight nod" where is Malik by the way?"

" he went out to get something, not sure of when he will return"

" ok"

" freshen up, I will see you outside"

" sure" she Watched Rebecca get off the bed and walk out of the room. She glanced at her clock. it was past 10. how come she slept for so long, rolling her eyes as she gets out of bed as well?

****

There was silence between the two as they walked awkwardly by the beach. Lara was beginning to get uncomfortable by the awkward silence, she caught Rebecca Stelling glance at her times without number and this gave her a strange feeling that something wasn't right. She noticed that they were in an unfamiliar part of the ocean and it was quiet, too quiet, filled with rocks. A good hiding spot for hide and seek. Not a single soul in sight but them. The sound of the ocean waves filled the air calming her nerves." uncomfortable?"

Rebecca finally said as she came to a stop. Lara stops as well and turns to face her.

" what makes you ask?"

" I can see from your body language. You are not comfortable"

" ha" she sighs

" I understand. All of a sudden I call you out for a walk and you think something is not right"

" I thought you hated me" with an eyebrow raised

" I won't lie, I do" Now she faces the water. Lara watched Rebecca walk toward the water. And sat on the sand very close to the water, sticking her legs out and as the water flowed, it washed her feet leaving them with particles of sand as it flowed back" but what can I do? Malik likes you and soon you will be my Lady, the chief's wife." she said still focused on the water. Lara decides to go join her, sticking her legs out as well, letting the water wash her feet, at first when the cold water hit her skin she tensed a little then relaxed almost immediately." calming right?" turns to her

" yes, it is"

"This used to be Malik and my favourite place" Rebecca says looking back at the water," when we were kids" she gave a small smile" We come here to get away from people and just relax. Back then I used to think that it was me and him against the world, nothing could separate us" there was a short silence between them... Lara could not focus on the water that washed her feet any more but on Rebecca. She stared at her for a long time until she finally broke the silence" I brought you because I don't have a friend to come here with. Malik and Cordelia used to be my only friends. Cordelia has gone back to school and Malik" she hesitates" You have gotten all his attention"

" I swear I didn't mean to break the bond between you two"

" you didn't do anything. Malik was never into me from the start" she gave a faint smile" I shouldn't be mad at you"

" you love him?" Lara finally said what she had been meaning to say" Don't you?"

" always have and always will"

" am sorry" feeling guilty. If the two were so close that they had a secrete hang out that meant, she was really getting in their way, now she understood why Rebecca wanted her to leave, but she couldn't, she loved Malik as well and not just Malik, she loved the place" I am so sorry"

" if you were sorry you would leave"

" I can't, I love this place" she says calmly" and I love Malik"

" that is why I won't regret what I am about to do" Her words got Lara confused

" what do you....." just like that it was like something hit her neck making her instantly dizzy, she struggled to turn around to see someone standing above her but she couldn't tell who it was due to the blurriness of the environment and the next thing she knows she was going down and she went blank.

****

Rebecca

"What took you so long" she says to Davina with a low tone looking around and hoping no one saw them.

" watch the way you speak to me" Sounding rude as always, Rebecca rolled eyes at her

" how will you carry her?" with curiosity in her tone. She watched Davina bring out her phone and dialled a number, it rang a few times before it was answered

" yes?"

" come now"

" yes ma'am" the call ended. A few minutes later, from behind, a yacht relived itself, driving towards their direction and it was a big one

" you own that ?" focused on the yacht

" yeah, why?"

" you writers do have a lot of money"

" focus"

" so what will you do with her?"

" that is my business" she says looking at the unconscious Lara, she bent down to adjust Lara's hair and a devilish smile made its way to her lips" I will end things today, once and for all" Her fingers explored Lara's face" to bad all this beauty will go to waste." at this moment Rebecca became curious about what Davina wanted to do with Lara, she began to re-think the whole, thing. Those words *too bad this beauty will go to waste* 'sounded like she was going to do something really bad

" what are you going to do to her?" she asked again looking down at Davina

" I said it is none of your business" she sounded upset this time" unless you want to come see for yourself self" she smiles. There was a long silence between the two and Rebecca didn't know when she replied

" yes. I want to see with my own eyes that she won't return" sounding very serious and Davina's smile widened

" I am beginning to really like you"

CHAPTER

16

Malik

"Home sweet home" Malik murmured as he entered the house. Taking the two steps down he walks to the sitting room" Love, am back" calls out to Lara as he places the paper bag he was holding on the couch. Took off his jacket and car key, throwing them both on the couch."Love" he calls out again but is responded to by silence" Is she still sleeping?" he lifts his hand and glances at his wrist watch" It's past 12" In a low tone" Is she sick?" worried. Immediately he made his way to her room." Lovett" knocked on the door gently" are you alright?" Malik turns the handle and opens the door gently only to find the room empty." Lovett?" he calls out but no response.

After returning from checking his library and study, he came to the conclusion that she had gone out. To town.

Malik sat on the couch and reached for his phone in his pocket. He dialled her number twice with no response" I have told her severally not to put her phone on silent, for goodness sake where is she" he frowned. He kept the paper bag on the floor and kicked his jacket out of the couch. Malik stretched his legs. Now he was lying on the couch with his eyes closed hoping to get a quick nap before Lara returns or before he gets a call from the lab.

Just as he was about to drift into the dreamland he heard the doorbell" Damn it" his attempt to take a nap had failed. Who could it be? There is no way it is Rebecca or Lara, they both knew the password. It can't be any of his family members. The doorbell rings again" give me a minute" Malik forced himself off the couch, making his way to the door. The doorbell rang again" for goodness sake I said give me a minute" he scolded the moment he opened the door and was taken by surprise by the person in front of him." Imran?"

"Sir Malik" panting like he has been running all day. There was this look on his face that made Malik feel uneasy, like something big had happened.

" what is it?" a sudden change in his tone as a sign of seriousness

" sir...sir Malik" panting" I..i think...Lady Guinevere is in danger" hearing this Malik steps out, standing over the child like he was going to ambush him that instant.

" what do you mean danger, what happened?" trying to keep calm not to scare the boy off

" I went to the back of the Island and I saw Sister Rebecca and an unfamiliar woman and a man carrying Lady Guinevere into a yacht. As if she was dead because I didn't see her move and her eyes were closed"

" oh my God" panicking at this point. Malik began running down the stairs, realizing he didn't have his car key he ran back up and grabbed it from the couch along with his phone. Then runs out again and down the stairs while the little boy watches." go the the house and tell my father what happened and tell him to send the search team out in the ocean." he instructed while running off to get his car.

" OK" Imran responded

****

Lara

Her head ached unbearably, and her body felt weak. From the background someone called" Lara" The uncertain voice sang to her" Lara wake up" it repeated. Lara struggles to open her eyes. What had happened to her? Why was she in so much pain?" Lara!" the voice snapped angrily this time.

Lara Successfully opened her eyes. her environment completely blurred at first but after a few blinks, it slowly began to hit her of where she was and what happened. In front of her stood Davina with a devilish smile" I hope you enjoyed your sleep because you are about to go for an everlasting one" she bent down to Lara's level to whisper.

" you!!" angrily and about to move when she realized that she was tied to a chair with hands tied backwards. She looked around to examine where they were and by the look of things, they were in

a yacht and surly in the middle of the ocean" What are you doing?"

" what does it look like am doing" Davina says while walking away, making way for Lara to see Rebecca leaning on the cabin with arms crossed the moment her eyes came in contact with Lara she looked down to avoid eye contact" You too?" shocked"but why?"

" don't ask me why like you don't know" She looks up again sounding angry

" no, I don't, enlighten me please"

" are you for real?" shocked at Lara's words" You really want to pretend like you don't know what this is about" There was silence between the two as she watched Lara trying to recall if she did anything wrong" You took everything away from me Guin" she yelled" what I have worked for all my life you appeared, out of nowhere and just like that you took everything like it was nothing"

" is this about Malik?"

" Yes Lara, it is about Malik OK" she yells and they both fall into silence. Rebecca sobbed" I have loved Malik since when we were kids, I have done everything in my power just to make sure we are always together, I even made sure we got into the same university and worked at the same place. I loved what he loved, wore the same perfume he wore, I learnt to play video games for him even his favourite food was my favourite food"

" what kind of sick obsession is that?" with pure irritation in Lara's tone

" call it whatever you want to call it Guin. All I am saying is that you took my chances with him away and I have tried to get over it but I can't, I just can't"

" so you decide to work with this phyco" Lara says" Davina?"

" shut the fuck up" Lara received an unexpected slap from Davina" You bitch" with a low frustrated tone" You still have no fucking idea what you did to me do you?"

" I did nothing" she defended" You destroyed your career with your own hands when you framed me for infringement" looking into Davina's eyes with full confidence" What I still do not understand is why you did it" sounding completely lost at this point

" you know Lara" taking a few steps closer to Lara" Of all the things I hated about you there is one thing I hated the most." she stops for a moment" The fact that you act like you don't know what is happening, what you are doing to people, you act clueless"

" I did nothing to you, Davina. We were friends"

" no we weren't" she yell in frustration" I took you as a friend but you never did"

" what do you mean?"

" you shut me out every time I try to have a conversation with you. You pushed me away like I was a nobody. When you first arrived I wanted us to work together, the two very best but you pushed me away like I was nothing, I came to your house and you locked me out"

" you came to my house unannounced and you know very well I don't like people around"

" I am your friend for goodness sake, or I was" sounding disappointed" at the office you spoke to me with no emotion, you and Mr James always left me out. In five years you won 8 Oscar awards while it took me over ten years to win 6. Just like that, you became my superior. People mocked me about it, the news carried it about on different occasions. Movie industries were always interested in Lara's work, every industry wanted to produce your film. Your books made it to the top sales while I was left alone like I never existed"

" that is a lie. You got your work sold out as well"

" but it wasn't enough. You were my junior and just like that I was out of the picture. And when we talk you act like you don't even know what is going on. I was your rival, I hated you, almost every worker hated you and you didn't give a shit about any of it. you made me feel like I was an idiot or something. You made me feel like a worthless piece of shit"

" you felt that way because you wanted a competition and I had no interest in your stupid competition. Not everything is a competition"

" everything is a competition!!!" raising her voice"and I love to win. But you didn't even give me a chance to start the race, you just went on like I was not worth your time"

A long silence between them. Lara never knew that not caring angered Davina. After all, Lara had gone through while growing up. She had learned to survive on her own. Not getting attached to people because people will betray you, not caring about what people think or say about her. She knew very well that she was surrounded by people who hated her, but she never paid attention the them and just moved on like there was nothing going on. She believed that, that way she would have peace of mind and also it had helped her to pay attention to what is important which is her career and that is why she has always been successful. But never did she know that people also hated her for not caring. Why are humans so complicated?

" I'm sorry" she finally said" I had no idea that I made you feel this way" she said with honesty" all I wanted, was to just be on my own and not get attached to people"

" then why don't you want to leave the island?"

" Because that island has shown me what it is really like to have people around, people that love you and will put a smile on your face" Lara says calmly" It gave me the family I never had"

" bullshit" Davina snapped." but I don't care" she glanced at her wrist watch" time is up" she smile and walked toward Rebecca's direction

" what will you do to me?"

" finish the job that the plane crash didn't finish" Rebecca's eyes fell wide open as she realized what Davina meant

" wait, that was you?" Davina ignored Lara's question and reached for the bag next to Rebecca. Rebecca watched in silence as She searched the bag and finally brought out a gun

"This is a MARK23. My father got it for me when I turned 20" she displays the gun

" wh...what are...you planning to do" Rebecca asked nervously, while Lara remained speechless

" what does it look like am doing" she smiles then she points the gun at Lara" making sure she doesn't return to that island and my life"

" this is not what I agreed on"

" I said what I do to her is my business" focused on Lara

" it is but not when I am the one who helped you to capture her" Rebecca stepped forward" I don't what her dead"

" when I told you it will be like she never existed. what did you think I meant?" rolling eyes at Rebecca

"maybe lock her up somewhere not kill her"

" will you shut the fuck up" she turns the gun at Rebecca in frustration, immediately Rebecca raised her hands in surrender" or I am going to kill you first then her?"

" no, no"

" you know one shot is all it takes" She gave that devilish smile

" am sorry. Just carry on. Do whatever you have to do, as long as she is out of my life"

" thank you" now pointing it back at Lara

" Davina, you don't want to have blood on your hands" trying to keep calm

"It's not like it's the first" Still smiling" Now, any last words" Lara remained silent. She couldn't

believe it would truly be her last day. When she finally had a reason to go on living, death showed its face" goodbye heart" Lara slowly closed her eyes when she saw Davina about to pull the trigger and" boom" the sound of the gunshot filled the air but Lara didn't feel a thing. She thought gunshots use to hurt, why can't she feel a thing" you bitch" she heard Davina scream frustratedly

"Don't do this" Rebecca's voice followed. Lara opened her eyes to see Rebecca and Davina struggling for the gun. She didn't expect it. why would Rebecca be helping her? A moment ago she wanted to get rid of her. Instantly Lara's survival instinct triggered. She has to free herself

****

Malik

Malik in his yacht with police officers. The search team had already gone out to the ocean in the search for Lara while they communicated with Malik's yacht. Malik was finding it difficult to stay calm, especially after what Imran said about Lara being dead. He said she wasn't moving. What if she was truly dead, What would he do? How will he take it? He will never forgive

Rebecca. Also, it was possible that she was just unconscious, he strongly believed that Rebecca was not capable of killing anyone.

" Malik do you copy? over" The walkie-talkie broke the silence in the yacht as it called out to the name of Malik's yacht. One of the police officers reached for it in a hurry

" yes we copy, over"

" I see a foreign yacht straight ahead, over" The person's words made Malik stand up and walk towards the officer

" is she in there? is she safe?" he spoke impatiently

" Have you confirmed her presence, over" the officer asked more calmly

" We are on it sir, over"

" search the yacht, we will be with you, over" Just as he was about to put down the walkie-talkie they heard the loud sound of a gunshot

"*boom*"

" that is a gun shot" Malik says to the officer in panic" that is a gun shot"

" what is the situation over" the officer asked the person on the other side"

" I think someone just realised fire. sir"

" you think?" Malik yells" you think?"

" sir Malik, calm down" the officer says to him

" I can't calm down, that could be Guin" he says as he increases the speed of the yacht. Saying to himself" *Lovett please be OK*" so low that only a vampire could pick up what he said

CHAPTER
17

Lara

While the two women fought over the gun, she struggled to free herself. Battling with the chair. Just then an idea hit her. She remembered something she always did when her father tied her up. Lara twist her hand from the back, turning it to the front and Damn, it was hurtful due to it being a while since she did it but she had no time to cry over the pain. Using her teeth to lose the endless knotting around her hand" fuck you" the gun flew out of both of their hand. Davina wanted to reach for it but Rebecca grabbed her leg resulting in a great fall and the two threw slaps and pouches at each other. It looked entertaining but Lara wasn't interested. Finally setting her hands free she unlashed the rope around her feet and stood up. She would have taken the gun but she had no interest in holding a gun she won't use. Davina kicks Rebecca in the face, about to reach for the gun again instantly Lara makes a run for it

" I think we are being followed" a man around his late twenties, with golden hair, greenish blue eyes, 6 feet tall, appears at the doorway." what the?" shocked at the situation" When you leave the job to a woman and......" before he could finish his sentence Lara's leg found itself in between his legs, crushing his balls" arrrrrr!!" falls in pain and she jumps over him to escape

" let me go, you bitch" Lara hears Davina yell at Rebecca.

Running out. There was nowhere to go. She was surrounded by water and didn't know if she would be able to swim. After her last experience when drowning, she wouldn't try swimming again. She could still hear the ladies struggle from inside. Running to the back to find a place to hide, that was when she spotted them. Several ships heading towards the yacht. Then she saw him. His yacht, *Malik.* She knew it was his because he had once told her about it and she mocked him for naming his yacht, *Malik.* He was coming for her. He was coming to rescue her. At that moment it was like she was finally saved.

" Lara" she heard Davina's voice before she could do anything. The sound of a gunshot filled the air again and echoed in Lara's ear"*boom*" Startled, Lara turned around to realize she wasn't the one who got shot, it was Rebecca. She was holding onto the gun when Davina released the trigger

" oh my god" Lara screamed in disbelieve as she watched in horror, blood came pouring out of Rebecca." no, no" she had watched in movies how people got shot, directed scenes of actors getting shot but never in her life had she seen someone get shot in reality

" let go!!!!!" Davina yells at the bleeding lady in frustration who refuses to let go and just like that Davina shoots" *boom*" her again like it was nothing. And again"*boom*"

" aaaaaaaaaaa" Lara let out another scream of horror. Davina pushed Rebecca's weak body out of the way.

" Now you" She points the gun at Lara but before she could pull the trigger that familiar voice echoed

" Lovett!!!!!!!!!!!!!!" it was Malik and it was followed by a gunshot that aimed straight for Davina's hand

" aaaaaaa' she cries in pain while the gun falls off her hand. Other gunshots followed, and immediately Davina left the gun, trying to save herself, she ran off into the yacht. Lara fell on her knees completely weakened by the horror of what she just saw. The world around her began to spin and blur. She just watched someone die, her friend just died and it was because of her. Even if Rebecca hated her, she just died trying to save her. Not able to hold back.

" a...a....a....aaaa..a.a." began to cry, finding it difficult to breathe. Holding both hands together crumbing in fear, she cried out loud. It has been years since she cried out loud, cried like a lost child. Lara had no idea what happened next, she didn't even realize that she was surrounded by officers until someone pulled her into his arm. Malik.

" I got you" holding her tight as she cried." am sorry" whispers to her ear" I am so sorry" whispering to her ear

" she.....she" not able to speak proper words. Two officers ran to Rebecca while the others went to search for Davina. With eyes on Rebecca, the look the men gave said it all. She was gone" aaaa!!!" her cry grew louder as she turned to hide her face in Malik's chest while his hug grew tighter

" Re... Rebecca" the name rolled out of Malik's lips so low that if it wasn't because she was this close to him, she wouldn't have heard. Lara heard the pain in his voice as he said the name and this made her heart hurt so much. It was her fault, she believed. His childhood friend was killed because of her

" I'm so sorry" she cried to his chest" I'm sorry I....sorry"

" shhhhhh" trying to calm her down" It's ok, it's going to be ok I promise"

****

" so I ran out and that was when I saw the ships and Malik's yacht and then......." Lara hesitates as she tells the story to the police officer while he takes notes. She was still traumatised but tried to hold on. Malik still had her wrapped in his arms as she spoke, making sure she was ok." she called my name.....and then.....and then.." the tears came flowing once again

" I think you have done enough Lady Guinevere" the officer said closing his notebook and returning his pen to his pocket" You need good rest."

" thank you very much officer Adam" Malik thanked the elderly man

" I should be the one apologizing for our carelessness. we had an intruder on the island and we had no idea" The man sounded guilty as he spoke" Please forgive Us Sir Malik" looking at the ground

" it's ok. What about the woman?" Malik asked curiously

" we will have to hand her over to the California Authority" he spoke sadly

" she killed one of us" Malik had a bit of anger in his tone which sent chills down the officer's spine

" I will make sure we get justice, sir. I promise you that"

" you may leave" he said. With that, the officer left the room. Malik looked down at Lara who stayed in his arms quiet. She was completely lost and he totally understood" I will make sure this never happens again, Love" he whispered

"It's because of me Malik. I caused her pain and in the end, she died trying to save me"

" Lovett. Listen to me" lifting her head so she would look into his eyes" it wasn't your fault OK? It wasn't" Lara looked away from him knowing that he was only saying that to console her, but what's the point?

" you only say that." the tears flow once again

" oh Lord... come on you need to sleep"

" I can't"

****

Lara didn't leave her room for three days since the incident. Malik has been busy with Davina's case and also the island was preparing for Rebecca's burial. Still blamed herself, if only she had left as she said in the beginning, then Malik's childhood friend would still be alive by now.

She always saw the sorrow in his eyes whenever he spoke to her, though he tried to fake being ok but everyone knew he wasn't.

heard a knock on her door and a frown made its way to her face. She had been inside her blanket all day and had told Malik not to come to her, she didn't want to see his face, it would only make her hate herself more." Malik leave me alone"

" why should we leave you alone" the door opened and the voice she heard took her by surprise

" Mother?" she lifts the blanket slowly to see Lady Thalassa standing there

" how are you, my child?" Lady Thalassa side walking towards the bed

" Mother..." she sits up trying to hold back her tears. suddenly the door opens again

" surprise" Cordelia jumped in

" oh my god, Cordelia ?" joy mixed with shock flashed in her eyes. Immediately Cordelia ran to her, climes the bed and pulled her in for a long warm hug

" I've missed you" she says into Lara's ear as they hugged

" me too" Cordelia pulled away to give her a proper look and the view in front of her was a disappointing one

" you look terrible."Cordelia breaks to her and she laughs weakly

" so do you" It was seen in Cordelia's eyes that she was also not doing well. Rebecca's death affected her" Malik told you, didn't he?"

" yes he did" looking down sadly" and he also tells me that you are beating yourself with it"

" and you are not eating" Lady Thalassa crossed her arms with a frown" You shouldn't play with food in times like this"

" I didn't have any appetite" playing with her nails like a child

" nonsenses" Lady Thalassa scold" I will go and prepare something for you and you will eat it whether you like or not. Cordelia, watch her for me" with that she walked out of the room

"Mother doesn't like it when we don't eat" Cordelia reminded

" I know" Nodding" I told Malik not to call her, I told him not to call anyone"

" it is a good thing he did. He told me that it happened right in front of you and you are finding it hard to recover"

" that is not it Cordelia." tears almost ran down her check once more" She died because of me"

" did you kill her?"

" no?" the question took her by surprise

" did you order her kill ??"

" no!!" getting irritated

" then how is it because of you"

" she....."

" as much as it pains me" Cordelia cut her off" We have to be honest. Rebecca messed up. She wanted to kill you"

" no she didn't, that is why she tried to protect me" Lara defended

" whatever. She wanted to get rid of you. And realized she was doing wrong and tried correcting it, but it was already too late, so none of it is your fault"

" she died trying to save me. All she did was because she loved Malik, and I took away her chances"

" Guin listen. Or should I just call you Lara now"

" no, I like Guinevere"

" ok. I want you to get out of this bed right now" Cordelia stood up" take a shower because it smells like you haven't had your bath in a week"

" That is harsh" frowning

"We go eat" she continued ignoring her" and get fresh air. Rebecca's burial is tomorrow night and we are going whether you like it or not" Lara sighs

" ok" reluctantly

" good, now get up" She struggled out of bed to go do as she was told

With a weak gone by. The Island still finding it difficult to recover from losing a very important member. Malik and Lara's relationship continued. Malik was still hurting but tried to be happy for the sake of his people, a leader has to be strong he believes.

Lara on the other hand has been taking Cordelia's Advice to stop blaming herself. After it was announced to the world that she was alive, reporters had been flooding the island, trying to interview her but they were always sent away saying she wasn't ready.

Lara finally concludes. She has to go fix herself, and her past. She has been running away her whole life, trying to get away from her past but it seems that her past didn't want to let go, she has to go face it, that is the only way she can move on in peace

" am home" Malik announced as he walked into the house and his nose hit an amazing aroma." Lovett?" he calls out

" in the kitchen" She replies with excitement in her tone. He made his way to the kitchen only to find Lara busy, cooking. This was the first time she cooked in his kitchen. The only time he sees her cook is when she assists his mother back at the family house but here she was wearing an apron, busy in his kitchen. She looked perfect" good evening" she greeted as she noticed his presence with a warm smile

" what about madam Tina?" asking for the whereabouts of the cook that comes In to cook for them most of the time when they decide not to eat out

" I told her not to come, I wanted to cook today" she walks past him holding a tray of covered dishes, heading for the dining" I wanted you to try out my cooking"

" what is the occasion?" following behind her with a confused and excited tone

" nothing just wanted to"

" haa" A gasp escaped his lips at the sight in front of him. She did a lot of cooking

" is it too much?" arranging the plate with the others '

" I don't know" holding back a smile, she walks to stand next to him

" I made a Nigerian dish and a few of your cultural dishes that mother taught me" she spoke nervously" I haven't cooked for anyone since my father" with a low tone" You are right on time to try them out"

" Okay..." he took off his jacket, placed it on the chair head, and sat down

" give me a minute" she runs to the `kitchen and comes back after a while with a jug of milk and two glass

" that is a lot of milk" he marked with his eyes on the jug as he watched her arrange them on the table, then sat down beside him

" have you ever heard of Nigerian jolof rice?"

" I have, but never have I tried it"

" ok, heads up" she smiled" I am a Yoruba girl and sometimes I like to take spice food"

" how spice can it be" he mocked

" ok" holding back her smile as she presented the food in front of him

" wow, this is an eye catch" he complimented as he reached for his fork,

Lara watched quietly. He took in his first spoon then paused" oh my God" with eyes wide open

" what!!" almost panicking

" This is good" using his spoon to point the food

" Really?" with an eyebrow raised

" yes"

" not spice ?"

" oh no, it is spice" nodding his head dramatically which made her laugh" but good" he continued eating

" try the next one" she says

" help me with the milk" with a mouth full while she laughed at his reaction to the pepper

" then stop eating" Handing the milk over to him, immediately he took a gap" So you can try the next" she repeated desperately

" ok" moving the food to the other side, Lara was about reaching for it but he held her hand back" what are you doing?"

" are you still going to eat that,"

" excuse me ?" dramatic" Yes" he moved her hand away"You can't give me something this delicious then take it away" Sounding like a child Lara burst into laughter once again.

" ok" laughing" try this one"

****

They carefully cleaned the place while talking about random things. Malik took the last plate to the kitchen while She cleaned the table. His phone began to ring from his jacket pocket" Lovett please help me with that" he called out from the kitchen

" sure" she grabbed the jacket and explored the many pockets for the phone when something suddenly caught her hand and attention. Bringing out a small blue box, She suspected what was inside but didn't want to jump to conclusions. If it was truly what she thinks it is then it won't be good. Lara slowly opened the box and was stunned by the beauty of the ring inside the box.

She stood there in shock not knowing how to react to the whole event about to take place. Malik plans on proposing soon, she thought to herself

" love?" Malik called out as his ringing tone died out" Love are you alright?" he hurried to the dining to see her standing still"Lovett?" he called, and she slowly turned around to reveal what she was holding. Seeing this Malik sighed in relief, for a moment he thought something had happened

" Malik?" calling for an explanation with a serious tone

" oh. That" robbing the back of his neck nervously" I know that we are getting married but I thought it would be nice to ask you properly. Lara remained still unable to say a word. He walks towards her and stops" I wanted it to be a surprise"

" I am surprised alright" in a very low tone, their gaze meet

" ok then" gently collecting the box from her" I guess I will just do it now" he smiles brightly about to go on the kneel immediately Lara stops him by grabbing his hand

" no, Malik stop!!" panting, confusing the young man

" what? Why?.. are you ok ?" not knowing the right question to ask

" Malik" their gaze meets once again. Malik noticed her hesitation making him worry

" what is it?" She remained quiet, just kept staring

" I am leaving" she finally brock" I am going back to California"

" oh. Well that is not a problem, I will prepare the pl....." she cut him short

" no Malik you don't understand. I am leaving and I don't know when I will be coming back, I can't say in a week time or month. I don't know" shaking her head

" what do you mean you don't know?" all that little happiness on his face drained" why are you suddenly leaving, you said you would stay, you will stay with me, with us" trying to put yourself together

" Malik" in a weak tone" I need some time to fix things. I choose to stay on this island to get away from everything but it seems like it keeps following me" she takes his hand" I have to go fix my relationship with people back in California, I have to see Davina and have a proper conversation with her, I have something important that I have to do in the industry, the press is already waiting to hear from me, I have to see..." she stopped and looked down" I have to see my father back in Nigeria" at that instant Malik became calm remembering the story she told him about her father

" do you have to?" he said

" I have to. I have to speak to him, I think that way I will finally have peace" she said and he could clearly see the pain in her eyes" and the nightmares?"

" I thought you said you no longer had them" almost upset about the fact that she lied to him

" I did but, they returned after the incident"" *Boom, boom*"the image of Rebecca getting shot replayed in her head and she flinched. Immediately he noticed, he held her hands tighter" and also, I want to find out about my real mother. What happened to her?" she says

" I see" calmly

" Malik I'm sorry" trying to hold back her tears" I know I promised and I am breaking my promise. I truly wa......" cuts her short

" Guinevere" he pulls her for a long warm hug" I get it"

" I think you should get someone to marry. It will be...."

" I will wait" cutting her short again" I will wait for you no matter how long it takes"

" but the people will ask questions"

" they will if I marry someone else sooo" whispering into her ear" It is you I want so I will wait" They remained like that for a while, in comfortable silence. If only she didn't have to leave. If only she will just remain like this in his warm arms. It felt perfect this way.

" what if I don't come back?" she says into his chest making him pull away to look her in the eyes

" Don't try it" he warned" I will come for you with this ring and holy oil"

" why oil?" holding back a smile with an amazed tone

" the oil will be used to wed us instantly. After putting the ring I will use the oil to draw a cross on your forehead, meaning you are now with me" instantly she let out a loud laughter

" you are not serious"

" we will find out then" he smiles

" Malik" the laugh faded replaced with seriousness" I will be gone for a long time"

" And I will wait"

" ok" hugs him again.

CHAPTER

18

Lara returned to California and went straight to the industry. where she is greeted by reporters. She gives them a little information and is finally rescued by securities in the industry. Lara makes her way for Mr James who stands by the reception area to welcome her"oh lord, Lara" he smiles brightly as he approaches her"

" Mr James" she greeted offering her hand for a handshake with a smile

" you have no idea how happy I am to have you back" holding her hand like a treasure" I have missed you so much"

" I know" nods slightly

" I can't believe that Davina did that to you. I always knew she was a devil"

" And you took her in during my absence?" she says making his smile fade away

" oh" finally letting go of her hand" lets take this to the office" he offers

" I agree"

they headed for his office while Lara took the workers by surprise with the way she responded to their greetings with a smile and not just any smile, a sincere smile.

" so tell me, how have you been?" he asked with concern in his tone. They were both seated in his office" I am sure you had a hard time on that island

" I actually had a great time. The island is a wonderful place for vacation"James who wasn't expecting that response nodded in disbelief.

" really? I have heard about how wonderful Marine Island is, I never believed it" he says" about Davina?" sounding guilty

" I am not interested in the things you do in your company" She crossed her legs against each other." Which includes the relationship you had with Davina" she spoke, sounding authoritative as she used to

" oh.. ok" relieved" so what are your plans"

" first." she began" You will hold a press conference. I have a lot to say to the press and I don't enjoy being stopped on the road for questioning. Then" she reached for her handbag and brought out a brown envelop, placed it on the table

" what is this?" with an eyebrow raised

" check it" She watched Mr James reach for the envelope, open it then pull out the papers" It is the treatment for my new story"

" oh really?" excitedly, he sits up

" read it and give me feedback." she says" and I want it as soon as possible so I can start working on the script"

" ok"

" and also, I will be going on a two-week break"

" already?" confused

" I am going somewhere important"

" where?"

" Nigeria" she breaks it to him. And his eyes fell wide open

" after your last experience?"

" that is my burden to carry not yours. Just get back to me" she stood up and he followed" by the way. My secretary?"

"The moment you told me you needed her I sent for her return."

" good. And also increase her salary, she does a really good job and she has a sick mum"

" how come I do not know that and you do?"

" I pay more attention than you think I do" smiling and making her way to the door

" Lara?" James called, stopping her at her track

" yes?"

" I like that smile of yours. It gives you this totally different aura"

" thank you" Smiling brightly before she walked away.

****

Lara made her way out of the office when that familiar, strawberry blond hair, ocean green eyes, and cute young lady began running her way. Joanna" Madam Lara" smiled brightly."I am so happy that you are back" sounding excited. Of all the people in the industry, Joanna was the one who gave her that sincere happy smile and she never knew why. Probably why she was her longest of all secretary" how are you feeling?" with a concerned look

" I'm fine" she began walking and Joanna followed behind her

" Mr James said you wanted to see me"

" yes" still walking

" what for?" Lara stops at her track and turns to the lady who stops as well

" don't you work for me ?"

" wait....?" filled with excitement" you mean I still got the job"

" I never fired you did I?"

" yes" she yells in victory, calling attention their way and this makes Lara smile" am sorry"

" no problem" she began walking again" now come with me"

" where are we going?"

" to jail" Lara said with reluctance

" pardon?" shocked

" to see a friend"

****

There was a comfortable silence between them as Joanna drove and Lara sat in the passenger seat scrolling through her phone. Updating herself on the thing she missed" I can't believe I missed the launching of, Black Adam, Wednesday, and Wakanda forever" Joanna turns to look at her in total confusion. Was Madam Lara speaking to her?

" oh, ammmm..... sorry?" not knowing what to say

" how is your mum?"

" pardon ?" more shocked than ever. she looks at Lara.

" your eyes on the road please" lifting her head to speak

" s...sorry" focusing ones again

" you once said that your mother had cancer" Lara reminded the young lady. Joanna never thought Lara would remember, she didn't even know that Lara had been listening to her. Maybe it was because of her reluctant response she always got." how is she doing?"

" well, she is still holding, fighting" Lara could sense the sadness in her response

" say hello to her for me" going back to her phone

" oh....ok" confused as to what was going on. Lara was really having a conversation with her. Did she hit her head somewhere on that island?

" Joanna ?" she called

" yes?"

" you told me you write" Instantly Joanna turned the steering, parking the car by the side of the road" Oh my God. What is the meaning of this" yells in fear of almost losing her life

" I..i... am sorry" smiling brightly" Yes, yes I do write" Lara stared at the lady for a while still trying to recover from the sudden event.

" I would like to see your work if it is ok with you. Maybe I can help you with one or......"

" yes!!" cutting her off excitedly" Yes I will love to have you read my book, I will be honoured"

" ok then" she smiles at the cute young lady

" I like that smile by the way"

" oh, thank you" smiled brighter" now can we continue our journey and please don't do that again"

" ok" she trying to hold back the overwhelming excitement in her tone" I'm so sorry"

****

"Attention passengers we will be arriving in the next 10 minutes" the pilot announced from the speaker. After so long, after 10 years she was

finally returning to Nigeria. She would never believe if anyone told her that she would return. A lot must have changed since she left. Will she still recognise her house? Will her father still be there? Lara takes a deep breath with her eyes closed. She could still feel the hatred towards her father, the anger inside of her grew stronger at the thought of seeing him again. There was no turning back. She has to do this once and for all

She arrived at Lagos at midnight. Spent the night and the next day she took a flight to Abuja. It was early October, at this time of the year, the weather is what one will describe as pleasantly warm, humid but cool. It was perfect for Nigerians but for someone who has stayed out so long. They will describe it as hot. She had to change into a white top and jeans. It is said that clothes with lighter colours help during hot weather.

Lara didn't waste any time going places. She sets out to find her father. Getting a Taxi driver who will drive her around town for the day.

Gwagwalada. She could never forget that place even after 10 years. The name of the place where she used to live with her father after he sold his house at Gwarinpa remained in her memory.

Getting to *Gwagwalada*She began describing the area but it was pointless. The place had become so different from 10 years ago. The only thing that didn't change was the bad road, in fact, the rain only made it worse. Lara expected the driver to get angry with the way she was taking him around town but with the amount of money, Lara offered to pay he didn't mind. In fact, he gave suggestions. Not every day does one wake up to have 50thousand Naira waiting for you just to be the driver for the day

" forgive me for all the stress. It has been a while since I left and the place has really changed"

" aaa... madam no problem" he smiled" Me self I dey sorry for you...if only you fit remember anything wey been dey popular for the place"

" I am trying" she said frustrated. She left the hotel at 8 am and it was past 2 pm with no luck

" may be like school or church..... or popular person where been live for the place" he said. With her eyes closed she leaned back in her seat and sighed in frustration

" Are you hungry?" asked, with her eyes still closed

" I dey fine ma"

" well me, I am hungry. Is there anywhere I can buy food" eyes, still closed

" like which kind of food"

" food. Good food" she now lifts her hand to massage her forehead" I honestly miss Nigerian food"

"They get this better restaurant where dey for that roadside" he pointed to the direction of the restaurant while She opened her eyes and leaned forward to look at what he was pointing" Me I no know whether you fit chop for that kind of place" he spoke honestly. It was natural for Nigerians to think that way about someone who comes from outside. Even with Lara's looks one will never believe that she is a Nigerian. She told the driver earlier and he found it hard to believe. She had to explain that she was mixed and her father is Nigerian.

" as long as the place is clean. I haven't eaten since last night" she says

" ok na" Lara watched him start the engine once again, driving onto the road, he drove for a while and stopped in from of the restaurant he spoke about. The restaurant didn't look fancy or classy, but it was ok. A nice clean building that says on the billboard just above the building *Halima's treats* and judging from the looks of things. There were not many people inside." it used to be very busy in the morning and towards evening. Now people don go work" he explained as they made their way in

" I like it this way"

" con, con here" he greeted loudly, informing whoever was to attend to them of their presence and he led her to a seat by the end of the room greeting people as they passed. Lara noticed the eyes on her, especially from the men and this made her feel insecure. It reminded her of when she used to work at a restaurant after running away from her father" trust me you will like the food" smiling at her and she smiles in response

" Good afternoon" a young girl around her early teens appears in front of them with an apron and a head tie, carrying a welcoming smile as she is greeted. It was clear that she was a Muslim and a beautiful one. She had a deep dimple and her eyes gave Lara a feeling of familiarity

" good afternoon" Lara replies smiling as well" how are you?"

" I'm fine thank you ma" she had a polite tone as well" What will you like to eat" asked with eyes on Lara, who didn't know how to respond

" watin una get" The driver assisted Lara

" We have rice and stew, Jolof rice, Jolof rice and beans, Eba, Tuwo and pounded yam"

" pounded yam please" she says. It had been a while since she had pounded yam, she wasn't even sure if she remembered the taste" what soup do you have?"

" Egusi, okkor, bitter leaf soup and ogbono soup" she listed

" Egusi please"

" ok ma"

" what about you sir" turns to the driver

"no me I am ok" he said

" why?" Lara asked curiously

" My wife dey put food for me for the cooler so when I am hungry I will eat it in the car"

" that is sweet of her"

" ok then. Please do you need anything before the food comes"

" no thank you" smiled softly

" ok"

Lara ate in silence feeling everyone's gaze on her. She couldn't tell if it was because she ate with a fork or because she didn't look like one of them. But the very person that had her attention was the young girl, whenever she came out to attend to customers." you sabi the owner of the place?" the driver broke the silence

" pardon?" lifting her head to look at him

" she just dey look you" he said using his mouth to gesture to the direction. Lara turns and by the door that leads to the kitchen she sees a woman, dark, slim, she also has a head tie around her head and she looks a lot like the young girl. Lara guessed that it was her mother. She seemed very familiar as well and the way the woman stared at her was different from the way others did. She had this stare like she was trying to figure Lara out

" I don't know and besides. Everyone here has their eyes on me" The Driver nodded in agreement" but you were right. The food is amazing"

"I talk am. Oya chop make we dey go" She finished eating and cleaned herself. Waiting for the girl to come over so she could pay. Instead, the mother did

" good afternoon sister" she greeted

" oh. Good afternoon"

" abeg. E be like say I know you but I don't remember from where"

" oh" she smiles looking up to the woman" I will also say the same to you too. You look familiar"

" I no fit talk say na school I know you from since you no be Nigerian but....." Lara caught her off

" I am a Nigerian." the woman eyes open in amazement

" eeeee" smiling brightly" Honestly you dey like all this black American"

" I get that a lot"

" watin you dey find for this place?"

" oh, not to worry I will handle myself"

" eeeey" nodding" no problem. But if you are looking for a house to rent or something like that, I can help. I have been in this area all my life" she said speaking more properly this time

" really?"

" yes now" gave a slight nod

" ok then, I am looking for a person" Lara sits up

"Who be that?"

" a man named Tosin, a Yoruba man, he should be in his late fifties by now" she explained and watched in silence as the woman thought

" does he have a child?"

" ammm....." Lara hesitated she didn't want to say her name but she figured that she would have to sooner or later. he is her father after all" he had a daughter. I mean" stops again" I am his daughter. Omorala Lovett Tosin" The moment the name rolled out of her lips the woman's face dropped and she stared at Lara in shock" They called him Baba Omolara back then and he......"

" use to drink a lot" she cut her off

" you know him?"

" Lara" her tone was soft and calm, filled with so much emotion" Lara is this you?" Lara stared at the woman for a while trying to remember where she knew her from"

" Halima ?" she stood up in shock as it hit her

" yes it is me Halima" Immediately tears ran down her cheek. Halima, how could she forget that girl? They were around the same age back then, they weren't friends but they were close enough. Halima was the one who advised her to sell her father's property so she could run away. The only person that offered to help but couldn't do much because she too had her issues with her family." Halima" With excitement the two pulled each other for a long hug

" oh my god. How did I not see it was you" she says. The two could feel people's eyes on them as if they were having a performance in the restaurant but they didn't care. Not even a little.

They spoke for a long time about a few things that happened in their life after Lara left. Halima's parent finally succeeded in giving her out for marriage and stopping her schooling but she was lucky that it was a good man she married. Halima breaks it to Lara that her father was arrested for robbery and released not too long ago and he is very sick.

****

Standing in front of that familiar red gate which was completely worn out. Lara flashed back to the first day they moved in after they sold their house at Gwarinpa and bought this smaller one. He promised back then he would make sure that things go back to normal and he would bring her mother back but things never got better, they only got worse. The house holds so many bad memories" are you sure you are ready to see him?" Halima spoke from beside her.

" yes. I have to. It is now or never" Halima pushed the gate open and entered while Lara followed behind her. In this old house, the paints were worn out, as well as the roof and walls. It seemed like the house would soon fall apart. It didn't use to be this bad. The environment was bushy but there were signs that someone cleans the place once in a while

" baba you dey house?" Halima called out but there was no response" Abi he went out" she thought out loud" But he no dey commot?"

"Maybe I should come another day" Lara said feeling overwhelmed by the different emotions taking over her. She was about to turn around when they heard movement. A man, a very old man holding a broom walking slowly. he had not a single hair on his head and although he was wearing a big top she could tell how skinny he was. Like his bones were going to cut through the cloths. And he will break any second. No one had to tell her who it was. Even with how terrible he looked, she knew it was him. Her *Father* after so long. There he was before her. The emotions inside of her grew stronger as she tried to fight back her tears.

He stopped at his tack noticing people's presence, lifting his head, his eyes fell on Lara and no one had to tell him It was his daughter. The child that he tormented for no reason. The child that he had supposed to show love but only gave her reasons to hate him. The child that he was so ashamed to see and the child who he knew, would never forgive him" La....Lara" he whispered the name

" hey" was all she could say as the two stared at each other for a long while." Halima. Sorry but can you please wait in the car with the driver. This won't take long"

" oya na" she left immediately.

" so how have you been?" gathering the courage to say something. After all, he could not do anything to her now. He didn't respond, just looking down in shame" I heard you were sick" she said" what is it?" he still did not say anything" is it HIV?" throwing another question" Or Cancer?" still no response"can't you talk?" frustrated by his silence" for God sake answer me" she yells

" a...,m......" he murmurs something to himself which angers her more

" can't you speak properly" scold

" I'm sorry" he said out loud like a child who's being scolded by his mother" I am sorry Omolara"

 Sorry?" with an eyebrow raised" Sorry for what?" she smiles but he doesn't respond" I see you don't know what you are sorry for?"

" for what I did to you"

" oh." her smile began to grow brighter like someone who's about to go crazy" What part ?" he remained silent again" What part?" she yelled" When you force me to drop out of school due to your drinking? Or when you left me hungry and came back only to beat me up? When you raped me countlessly?" screaming. Lara didn't plan for things to go the way it was going. She wanted to show him that she was ok, that what he did to her did not kill her instead it made her strong not show how frustrated she was" or is it sorry for not taking care and protecting your daughter as a father should? Or is it for using those words *You know I love you* whenever you hurt me?!!!!" she screams

" Lara...."

" don't you dare call my name"Cutting him off, her voice became calm once again" Do you have any idea how you almost ruined my life? Even after I left, I never had peace, nightmares haunted me, and I hated men for a long time. Was always insecure, always scared. I had PTSD if you even know what that is. The people I worked with hated me because I didn't want to have anything to do with them just because I was scared" the tears finally ran down her cheeks

" Lara I hate myself as much as you hate me and I regret everything that I did"

" cut the bullshit" she says" You don't regret a thing" Lara watched him slowly take a few steps closer. His body crumbled with every movement, and as he drew too close she immediately stepped back" don't get close to me" he fell on his knees in front of her" what are you doing ?"

" Lara. I know you will never forgive me for what I did. And I can't even leave long to make up for what I did and...." she cut him off

" just die." she says finally letting out the hated" I will forgive you when you die. So just die and I don't care how you do it. This earth no longer has space to accommodate you so just die" with that she pulled the gate open and walked out leaving her father who was now in tears on his knees. Finally, she felt relieved. She poured it out. She told him what she wanted to tell him all this while. She finally stood up to him and made him beg for forgiveness. Lara made her way to the car and she drove off with Halima in an awkward silence.

Miya Kwen

CHAPTER

19

Lara returns to California in two weeks. Before leaving she assigned a nurse to watch over her father after the test results came out saying that he had Adenocarcinoma (lung cancer) which was already at the last stage. She also paid to get the house renovated and asked Halima to keep an eye on him.

" I can't believe you want to direct once again after a long time" Joanna spoke while she folded Lara's clothes into the travelling bag. Lara sat on the bed taking note of things that needed to be done and things that had already been done during the pre-production process. Her script titled" *Island, Fate & Love"* already approved and ready for shooting. The major cast was set, the main locations had been gotten just a few minor needed, crew member was set and Lara was the director of the film. Once again after a long time of directing.

" why can't you?"

" you know. You kind of announced to the press 4 years ago that you would quit directing and all of a sudden you are directing a movie again? People are very curious about what is going on in your head" Lara lifts her head to give her a not approving glance" am sorry that was too informal" she apologized instantly. With the two growing closer, sometimes Joanna speaks without realizing making Lara irritated at times

" I wanted to do it again" looking down at what she was doing" Is something wrong with that?"

" not at all" replied quickly. Lara suddenly gets a text. She reached for her phone and paused after seeing the name that popped up. *Malik.* Since she left, Malik has been texting her to know how she was doing. She replies a few times but most time just smiles at the text. She wanted to call him, she wanted to hear his voice after such a long time but thinks she still needed time. Especially now that she had a film to direct, she couldn't risk any distraction.

" who is it?" Joanna interrupts

" no one" putting the phone aside

" Have you prepared my schedule for the week?" she asked

" I'll send it to your email" she zips the bag and sat on the bed watching Lara work. After a long while, Lara smiles, then she underlines a few sentences

" done" she lifts her head" have you booked our flight ?"

" yes. We leave tomorrow at 6"

" Good, so we are done for the night"

" that means" she stops" I can leave ?"

" yes" nodding

" ok" she stood up" You know I can just spend the night if you want"

" No I don't" Lara said without giving it a thought

" oh" turning around to leave but turning back once again" Don't you get lonely in this house alone?"

" no, I don't. I enjoy the silence" she says

" ok then. I will take my leave" reluctantly" but what......" Lara caught her off

" do you want to spend the night?" Lara asked while rolling her eyes

" yes. Yes I do"

" alright. It is late anyway" that was her final answer before leaving the room

" yes" Joanna whispers in excitement, throwing her fist into the air

****

A Year & three months Later

Lara receives an Oscar for Director of the Year for the hit film" *Island, Fate & Love"*. Making friends with the actors on set. She clicked with everyone on set faster than she thought that she could. Once again she made it to the top. Things were finally changing for her. no more nightmares, all that feeling of anger and hatred were gone. She finally forgave her father but still couldn't bring herself to go see him. She had more peace now and tried to do things that made her happy but there was something that she had made up her mind that would never change and that was men trying to have an affair with her. Some men will be men. She thought. And then there is Malik. The way he texted her reduced and this made her believe that he had finally given up on her. The thought of it made her heart ache every once in a while. She wanted to call him, hear his voice, she wanted to see him" *But it is too late"*he may not even look her way after this long, after ignoring his text, even the one time he called she didn't respond because she was on set. He may have gotten over her, she believed. She missed that Island, she missed the people, she missed Malik.

****

" focus on developing your character" she advised Joanna who sat on the couch next to her. She just finished reviewing her story

183

" I see"

" it is like you are putting more energy on what is happening around them and not the character. We have to know who this character is" she says with eyes on the paper" right now, for all we know about the male lead for example, he is 35 years old, blond, blue eyes who falls in love with a lady at first sight"

" ok" nodding

" then in the whole story you only focused on what is happening, you didn't tell us what he is like. As you tell the events also tell us about him, does he have anger issues or gets irritated easily. Or does he have any allergies, or any past stories, like an accident, for example, he lost his family and is still finding it had to recover. his personality, too nice or too honest may be. Let us know who he is"

" ok"nodding

" but all in all. Your idea is great, I love your plots and the setting."

" I have improved"

" I noticed. Very creative of you" she complimented

" thank you"

" well that is it" she stood up placing the papers on the table." In no time you will be writing great scripts"

" I was thinking of writing one for a movie. For a change" she says

" Good idea" nodding" Maybe you should join me on the one I am working on, I will be needing fresh ideas. Or you can just write yours"

"No" shaking her head" oh my god I would love to work with you" she stood up in excitement

" ok" with that Lara walked away

" damn, I am hungry." Joanna says to herself.

****

" Joanna would you like to go out for......." she stops noticing the room is empty"Joanna ?" calls out but no response" Where did she go already?" she reaches for her phone and dials the number, watching it ring as she waits for response. then she heard the doorbell" Who is it? ' she called out" Joanna did you let someone through the gate?" she shouted while walking towards the door wondering who it was. With the phone still ringing Lara opened the door and was taken aback by the person standing in front of her.

There he was. That deep ocean blue eyes, dark long hair all the way to his shoulders, perfect smile that could brighten anyone's day, and perfect figure.

" hi" his voice played in her head like a melody

" Malik.." in a very weak tone. Her phone fell out of her hands due to how much it was crumbling and her heart raced almost out of her chest

" oh" surprised holding back his laugh" your phone"

" oh ammmm" about to go down but Malik raced her to it. Picking up the phone his eyes scanned it

"The screen is ruined" he informs as he hands it over to her. It took Lara a while to finally collect the phone. They remained staring at each other for a long while in silence until" may I come in?" breaking the silence. He seems very calm, unlike her

" oh...ammm..yeah...yes" making way for him to enter" She watched in total loss as he entered the house using his eyes to explore the place

" nice place you got here" turning around, he then finally stops to face Lara who still stood by the door looking at him. He could see the shock in her eyes and he noticed she was trying to hold back tears

" what are you? Why are you? I mean how did you know I lived here"

" I told you I will come for you if you stay too long" he smiles

" but..." not knowing the question to ask" it has been a year. Ignored your text and calls and you still...."

" I told you I would wait and if you take too long I will come to get you"

" you waited?"

" yes, I did. I guess they were right when they say people do crazy things for love" he spoke as calmly as ever. She missed that tone of his" I love you Lovett" he says looking straight into her eyes. The tears she held back finally broke free as she rushed to him for a warm long hug

" I've missed you Malik" said into his chest

" I have missed you more" She missed him, she missed everything about him, his smile, his warmth, his voice that had the power to calm her down, his cute side, his authoritative tone when he gave his people orders, his play with his mother and sister. She missed his silly argument with Cordelia. They finally pulled away and she watched him reach for his jacket pocket and bring out that familiar small ring box, making her smile." be my wife Lara" he said" please"

she didn't hesitate" Yes... yes, I would" smiling brightly. She watched Malik gently put the ring on her

" perfect" he whispers, slowly kissing her hand" oh right" remembering something. Lara watched him search his jacket pocket and brought out a small transparent bottle which had some kind of liquid inside

" what is that?"

" holy oil" Lara almost confused, instantly remembered their last conversation

" what if I don't come back"
" Don't try it" he warned" I will come for you with this ring and holy oil"
" why oil?"

" the oil will be used to wed us instantly. After putting the ring I will use the oil to draw a cross on your forehead, meaning you are now with me"

she busts out into laughter at the memory

" I can't... believe you... seriously brought that" laughing

" you thought I was joking ?"

" yes," slapping his chest" you are such a joker" still laughing while Malik watched with a smile on his lips noticing that her smile had grown brighter than ever during his absence. It means she achieved what she wanted to achieve. he was so proud of her

" I saw your movie" cutting her laugh short" it was about out island"

" was it that obvious" nervously

" it was. I never knew you liked the island that much that you had a film for it and you made it magical"

" you have no idea" she says" I have missed you, and the island and mother and Cordelia and Anahita"

" they are waiting for you" looking her in the eyes" they are waiting for you to come back"

" they are?" overwhelmed by the feeling of being loved

" come back with me Lara" using his tomb to rob the back of her hands" My father is also waiting for his grandchildren" reminded and he noticed her blush even in her dark skin, he always noticed. His eyes fell on her lips. Those lips that he had been longing to take, waiting so long and now she was before him. Lara felt the sudden change of atmosphere and where his eyes were. She grabbed him by the collar, pulling him down to her level and their lips met. Perfect.

****

Lara's POV

Was this it? The happy ending that they always talk about. Was this the feeling? But what comes next? Is this when they say *they lived happily ever after?* This can't be our happy ending.

I guess I agree with Malik, it is what follows, that will be our happy ending. The happy, sad, easy, difficult, joyful and sorrowful times that will come and how we will go through it together. That is our happy ending.

THE END.

Miya Kwen